INSIDE THE
MADHOUSE
and other tales of delirium

Stephen Hernandez

www.stephenhernandez.co.uk

Book Layout © 2017 BookDesignTemplates.com

Inside the Madhouse / Stephen Hernandez. - 1st ed.
ISBN 978-1-9161126-1-2

Dedicated to Gavin Chappell and *Schlock! Webzine*, who let me begin to dream.

"I became insane, with long intervals of horrible sanity.

—Edgar Allan Poe

CONTENTS

DR. KIM

Doctor Kim was insane. The soldiers all knew it and the prisoners had no need to be told. At least *they* were spared the indignity of having to be confronted with it on a daily basis.

Captain Okinara had no such luck. And he cursed it daily.

Under the bleaching glare of the surgery lamps, the captain stood rigidly at attention whilst observing the doctor's every movement with a distaste bordering on loathing. The doctor, caught up in his work, as usual, seemed oblivious to the officer's presence, let alone his hostile scowl.

Prior to every surgery Dr. Kim personally supervised the cleaning of the operating theater. He was as excruciatingly precise and methodical in his surgery preparations as he was with everything. Today he seemed even more punctilious than usual.

The doctor had spent the last forty minutes bent nearly double, examining the meticulously polished and sparkling chrome fittings of the operating table. He seemed to be searching for something. His painstaking investigation was finally rewarded. He straightened up triumphantly and ordered one of the kowtowing staff nurses to remove an offending minuscule pinpoint of blood he had discovered embedded deep in the ratchet of one of the levers.

The doctor's, high-pitched, whining admonition was thankfully muffled by his face mask. The speck of blood would probably not even have been visible to the naked eye.

A human naked eye, that is. Dr. Kim wore specially modified spectacles strapped to his head, combined with extended telescopic lenses that had matched pairs of specially ground prisms that could be manually rotated so as to control precisely the angles and degrees of extended vision. It was his own invention. A bulky, unwieldy contraption that made him look like he was peering through binoculars from the wrong end. It gave his already skeletal and pinched features a bizarre, reptilian look.

He then bent over to examine the freshly sterilized instruments that had been placed on a tray next to the operating table. These were not the normal instruments that one would expect to find in a hospital surgery. They were sparse and crude, mere workmanlike tools, designed for speed and not delicacy, more suited to a field or triage unit on a battlefront. Although, in all fairness, it would have been difficult for a layman to know the difference.

There were however some clearly recognizable tools, even to a layman: a circular electric saw, known as the "Stryker saw," and a large pair of "Eslander rib shears." Even a layman might guess these were usually used in post mortems and not on live patients. In conjunction with these macabre tools, and in spite of all the sophisticated equipment at his disposal, the doctor only used battlefield triage instruments despite the fact that he only operated on live, unwounded civilian patients! This was all part of the doctor's supposed military research. The captain always wondered what the research was meant to accomplish—he had still not figured it out.

The doctor turned his myopic gaze on one of the guards and ordered him to bring in the patient. Captain

Okinara stiffened. The murderous physician always had the gall to call them patients! The guard clicked his heels smartly and marched mechanically out of the room to perform his duty. The captain grunted quietly to himself in approval. He knew how much his men hated the tasks they were ordered to perform, but they never lacked discipline.

Okinara remained where he was, as silent and stiff as a marble statue, staring into space and trying not to let the repugnance he felt for the fastidious little man in front of him show on his face.

The unconscious "patient," a dark-haired Caucasian male child of some eight years of age, was wheeled in and transferred from the gurney to the operating table by the theater staff. The anesthetist checked the boy's vital signs, inserted various cannulas, and connected the cardiac monitor and a breathing tube.

The doctor had by now scrubbed-up in the small adjoining room, and after being helped into his gloves by one of the nurses, he returned to the theater. He carefully examined the child's naked, unblemished body and then turned to the captain.

"Please have your men escort in the prisoner," he squeaked in his nasal falsetto.

The captain nodded to two of the guards. They marched out of the room and returned with the struggling prisoner—the boy's mother. She had been gagged, but it did not prevent moans and sobs from escaping her throat when she caught sight of her child lying pale and motionless on the table.

The soldiers secured her hands and feet to iron manacles set in the wall. She did not offer any kind of resistance; her eyes were fixed on the body of her son on the operating table. The nurses then placed the woman's head in a protruding adjustable vice also set in the wall, another of the doctor's innovations. The device, a kind of mechanical brace, prevented the prisoners from moving their heads so their line of sight was trained directly upon the operating table in the center of the room. Furthermore, to prevent any chance of the prisoners shutting their eyes, their eyeballs were fitted with eyelid fasteners so that they could not be closed. This meant that they were unable to blink so a nurse would occasionally drip an eye solution into the irises to prevent the misting caused by watering and dab them with cotton wool to dry the prisoner's tears.

The prisoner had no choice but to look directly upon the macabre and brutal scene unfolding on the operating table. To complete the prisoner's immobilization a leather muzzle that smelled of rancid saliva was tied around the woman's mouth to muffle any screams that might disturb the doctor in his work.

The Captain had witnessed countless 'operations' but today's procedure was particularly poignant to him. He had received a letter that morning from his sister in Osaka and she had enclosed a photograph of his nephew in his new school uniform.

He was proudly holding up to the camera a toy sailing ship that the captain had sent him as a birthday present. He was the same age as the boy on the operating table and looked remarkably similar. They both had plain, honest, and well-meaning peasant features.

The captain's sister had jokingly enclosed another photograph with his nephew dressed in a smart navy blue sailor's costume, but there was no mistaking the look of pride in the little boy's eyes to be wearing a uniform like his illustrious uncle. The young boy was not to know that the captain was usually dressed in dark green fatigues with the minimum of rank insignia. The boy stood ramrod straight at attention with his hand to his cap in an earnest attempt at a salute

The captain felt an unseen hand clutch at his heart. He bit his tongue.

A nurse slid a rubber brick under the back of the young patient causing the boy's arms and neck to fall backward and pushing his chest up towards the doctor's waiting scalpel. The next moments were scenes reminiscent of a butcher's shop, but a butcher's shop where the butcher had gone insane.

The doctor worked at a frenetic pace. It looked to all intents and purposes as if he were desperately attempting to save the boy's life but, in fact, nothing could be further from the truth. He made quick, deep incisions starting from the top of each shoulder and running down the front of the chest to the sternum and then he made a single, deeper horizontal slash across the stomach. The intrusion of the scalpel on the unblemished young flesh seemed unnatural and obscene, but what followed was even more terrible.

He used the saw and the shears to cut through the ribs at the sides of the chest cavity. This allowed him to lift the sternum and the attached ribs as one plate revealing the horrific sight of the lungs and still beating heart. It was physically hard work and the nurse was constantly mopping his brow. He was oblivious to her attentions. He was being particularly careful not to damage the pericardial sac which would have brought the whole operation to a premature end. Using the scalpel he removed the soft tissue still attached to the posterior side of the chest plate. Now all the organs were exposed. He set the chest plate aside.

At this stage the doctor would usually decide which technique he would use to remove the organs. Whichever technique he used it would always be done in a prim and systematic fashion, devoid of sentiment or feeling, characteristic of the man performing it.

Dr. Kim usually preferred to use the Ghon method. As opposed to the Letulle method, where the organs were removed *en masse,* with the Ghon method, they were removed one by one. It was a method usually reserved for the autopsies of infants and was rarely practiced on the living. Sometimes, the doctor would accompany each procedure with a lecture to his attentive subordinates, explaining the different methods he was using and why. Not that the *why* ever made any sense to the captain. Tonight the doctor was silent.

The mother's devoted eyes widened in stupefied disbelief as the doctor proceeded to remove the boy's vital organs and tie off veins and arteries to prevent excessive bleeding. The doctor had frequent whispered conversations with the anesthetist and checked the various monitors for the boy's life signs. The operating theater now stank like the abattoir it had become.

Ostensibly, the doctor's work was important for the war effort because he was researching transplant and surgical procedures that would improve survival rates of troops wounded on the front line and requiring emergency surgery. There were no adult male enemy prisoners to experiment on as the Army did not take prisoners, but there were a great number of civilian children and women in the occupied territories that could be used for such research.

The reason for manacling the mothers to the wall and forcing them to watch their children being mutilated alive and then, their organs removed and discarded along with their lifeless bodies was a mystery. It seemed it was the doctor's own private psychological experiment. And because of the cutting-edge surgical techniques he'd discovered, he was allowed a certain leeway. The authorities tended to turn a blind eye to his sadistic idiosyncrasies.

The doctor was careful that the mother, who had passed out several times, and been revived by the medical staff should not miss any of the organs he extracted. He would carry them over to her and hold them out to her like an obscene offering in a ritual sacrifice before he plopped them unceremoniously into a large, blood-stained chrome bucket.

Mercifully, for the captain, the "operation" was coming to an end. The mother lurching in and out of consciousness had gagged and vomited several times and the nurses had attentively cleaned the front of her gown. She now hung limply from the manacles at an odd angle, like a marionette whose strings had been randomly cut.

Dr. Kim approached the woman on several occasions towards the end of the operation and stared intently into her eyes as if searching for something. The prisoner had tried, unsuccessfully, to turn her head away, with the obvious abhorrence anyone would feel for the monster, but as the operation progressed towards its inevitable, lethal conclusion, her eyes became glazed, as if her natural reactions had been dulled and anesthetized as much as those of the "patient." The doctor's demeanor expressed no disappointment at this lack of reaction; in fact, the captain could have sworn he might even have been pleased. He went back to his repertoire of disembowelment with no obvious haste or lack of enthusiasm.

Dr. Kim always left the heart until last, as if he knew, that the mothers would tenuously cling to the hope that this still beating organ meant that there existed a faint chance that her child might survive the vivisection.

Before proceeding with this final surgery he looked once again intently into the eyes of the prisoner but as before they betrayed no emotion and might just as well have belonged to a corpse.

The captain was glad to see that the doctor had nearly finished. The child's grasp on life was now very tenuous indeed and the bleeps from the electrocardiograph were becoming more irregular. Thankfully the ordeal would soon be over and the child's wrecked and defiled body could be at peace. The theater was filled with the iron stink of blood. It was everywhere. The bucket was a terrible sight and was now very nearly full of discarded organs. From where he was standing, the captain could just see the exposed heart within the child's chest cavity, which was still beating, but only very slightly.

The doctor paused for a moment as if collecting his thoughts. Then, with swift, decisive movements, he cut out the still-beating heart and held it up triumphantly in his gloved hands. He walked over to the woman and peered yet again into her eyes to see if this had provoked a reaction. There was not a flicker of emotion from the woman. Dr. Kim tossed the heart disdainfully into the already full chrome bucket. It made an obscene flopping noise. The theater was eerily silent as if this last abomination had stilled the air itself. The strange calmness that had overtaken the room was disturbed by the sound of bleeps flat-lining on the machine. He strode over to the woman and pressed his face close to hers, almost within touching distance. She did not flinch. He remained frozen for a moment; his thin cruel lips twitched slightly. It was the first time the captain had seen the doctor display any sort of emotion—and worse, he could have sworn it was the beginning of a smile.

At this point, the doctor would usually order the captain to take the prisoner outside to be summarily executed. The mothers would then be buried alongside the remains of their children in the small graveyard at the rear of the camp. But today was different. Today he ordered her to be taken to his quarters. The captain opened his mouth to say something but then thought better of it. You didn't argue with the doctor.

Captain Okinara returned to his office and the permanent bottle of sake he kept in the bottom drawer of his desk. He took out his sister's letter and again looked at the photo of his nephew. He traced the outline of the smiling boy's face with his fingertip as he took a large swig of the wine.

He was disturbed by whatever reverie he had retreated into by a vigorous knocking on his door. He commanded, rather than asked, whoever it was to come, annoyed that his free time should be disturbed. A guard opened the door and ushered in two people. The captain's jaw dropped. It was Dr. Kim and the female prisoner. The doctor had changed into a formal suit. The woman was wearing a fresh white gown. She still appeared to be in a kind of somnambulant shock. The doctor was holding her hand.

Dr. Kim stepped forward and placed a very small box on the desk. The captain stared at the box for a moment and then reached across and opened it. There were two simple gold rings inside—a man's and a woman's. Wedding rings. For a moment, the captain could do nothing more than continue to stare at the box and its contents. Then he started to laugh. For some reason, Captain Okinara found he could not stop laughing.

THE WAITING LIST

I was diagnosed with liver cancer on Monday, July 7, 2002, at 4.45 in the afternoon. I looked out the surgery window as the doctor gave me the news. It was cloudless and sunny outside. People were walking past the hospital in shorts and Hawaiian shirts, happy to feel the sun on their backs, whilst this man in a tailored suit quietly told me the reasons for my death sentence—hepatocellular carcinoma, HCC, or liver cancer to you and me. The Big C. I had three months.

Afterwards, a male nurse escorted me to a ward where I was to spend four days undergoing fitness tests to see if I would survive a liver transplant. A long shot, I was told, but my only chance of survival, if there was one. After the four days, they decided I was fit enough. I wasn't particularly surprised at that; after all, keeping in shape was necessary in my line of work. I was put on the liver transplant waiting list. I went home.

My job was, of course, severely compromised. Not that I really do what would be termed a normal job with normal hours. You see, I'm a collector of sorts; I collect money. More specifically, I collect money from people who owe money to the wrong people.

Unfortunately for me, given my present situation, the working hours are extremely irregular. I'm expected to collect said owed dosh in a very short space of time, usually in fact, straight away. The people I work for are not in the habit of sending polite reminders. I am given a name and an address, and off I am expected to bloody well trot and bring back the necessary. Being on a twenty-four hour, seven-day-a-week, transplant waiting list for a new liver, with fifteen minutes notice to prepare yourself to be picked up by an ambulance, and rushed to hospital, severely compromised my ability to carry out said task to the satisfaction of my employers. They were not known for being sympathetic to organ failure of any kind unless the organ failure had happened after and not before they had been successfully reimbursed by the owner. And you see, I also, unfortunately, owed them money myself. Luckily, in my case, a compromise had been reached some time ago in which I had agreed to collect what was owed to them by other unfortunate mugs, and they, in turn, agreed to knock five per cent of the money I collared off of my debt.

I asked as humbly and politely as I knew how for a year's leave of absence so that I could remain at home as much as possible in the hope that I would receive the call from the hospital which would mean my salvation. I didn't tell them about the cancer and that I had been given just three months to live. In their eyes, this would have made me a financial liability, and they would have dealt with me accordingly. Instead, I told them I needed a bit of a rest to sort my head out as the job was getting to me. So, they gave me a compromise. If I didn't choose to collect the money from the person who owed it there and then when I was told to, I could instead provide the money they owed myself. I suppose it was fair enough given the alternative. After all, it did give me more of an incentive to collect the money.

I still had some years left to pay off my own debt. I was lucky because they had left me with all my limbs intact and my organs in the places they were meant to be, that is, still inside my body. What it meant, though, was that if just a few unrecovered debts were added to my own, I would be working for them for the rest of my life, or what little was left of it. My own debt was the last thing I had on my mind, though. It was time that was paramount to me. When you have been told you have X amount of time to live, time itself takes on an added solemn weight, and the ticking clock and the second hand on your watch become your enemies, remorselessly counting down the minutes and seconds you have remaining on the planet. However much I sometimes disliked life, I did not much relish an unknown alternative; from what I did know of it, no one else seemed that keen to find out any too soon either.

The waiting list for livers worked in a strange kind of way based on blood types and body weights, and naturally, subject to availability. So, you would think that having a common blood group like mine (O positive if you're asking) would be an advantage as there would be more livers available, but no, it worked the other way around: because it was a common blood type, it meant there were more people on that particular list. In fact, the list I was on meant that at the current rate of transplants for O positive patients, I would be looking at a wait of one and a half years. And I only had months, not years. The cancer was spreading at an alarming rate. Evidently, cancer tumors need a rich blood supply, and having made their bed in my liver, the tumors were reproducing so fast they could roll over, rearrange the pillows, and smoke a post-coital cigarette.

It felt like I was in a no-win scenario playing out my own personal end game—all very depressing. But I have never been a quitter. As the saying goes, "*When the going gets tough, the tough get going,*" or in my case, they get a liver.

So, I looked for a solution. There had to be an answer; there always is. If I couldn't get a transplant straight away, then the obvious thing to do was to improve my chances as much as possible; in other words, I had to change the situation to my advantage. As I may have mentioned previously my employers were not particularly concerned about the physical condition of the payee once they had paid back their debt. In some cases, they positively welcomed mortality, as this usually acted as a form of added incentive for others to settle their debts promptly. It occurred to me that I could kill two birds with one stone—quite literally, in fact. Get the money for my employers and improve my chances of getting a transplant by supplying fresh organs.

I would have to make sure the subject was not too damaged in the abdominal region. The liver had to remain intact. Hopefully, this would greatly improve my chances on the waiting list. Of course, the debtor would have to meet certain criteria: about the same weight as me, obviously the same blood type as me, and not have subjected their liver to substance abuse, which was quite common in some of the wasters I collected from. The main criterion was that the person would have to be dead. But that, as they say, could be arranged. I drew up a list of qualities that in my opinion would constitute a good donor and meet my own particular requirements. I was pleased with the results.

It was a while before a suitable candidate showed up. Most of the others were addicts of some sort or another. I didn't like to think about what state their livers might be in. But my fifth client looked good and met with my approval. He was young and buff. I was pleased to note he was a non-smoker as well. I roughed him up a bit first - that goes without saying - just to let him know I meant business, and then waited patiently whilst he rang his friends desperately pleading for funds—the usual "carry-on," in other words. He managed to get it all together in the end; they usually do. After all, as I'm fond of repeating, "The alternative is not pleasant." And in between my persuasive knuckle-dusted fists and boots, I was giving him plenty to ponder about what the future might hold if he didn't come up with the goods.

We finally ended up back in his flat after collecting all the dosh: a well-furnished bachelor pad in Chepstow, which coincidentally, was also quite near the hospital in charge of my transplant. It wasn't going to get much better than this. After I had put all the cash safely in my briefcase, I got out my donor questionnaire. Understandably, the guy was a bit taken aback by this. I suppose, he thought, our business completed, I should be on my way and not asking severely beaten punters to fill in questionnaires.

I made him complete it despite his protests and increasingly urgent enquiries into my mental condition. People as a rule, don't argue with me. There was one point he was not clear on, and that was his blood type. Considering the amount of it he had lost over the past hours, you would have thought this was something he really ought to have known. I just gambled that he was O positive the same as me. It was the most popular blood type, and it's usually only people with rare blood types that know them anyway.

It didn't take much to finish him off. I had made sure during the whole softening-up process to avoid any direct blows to the liver area. Now it was a question of getting the cadaver to the hospital as quickly as possible. Time was of the essence. I put him near his front door so it would be easier for the ambulance crew, the organ donation form I had made him sign clearly visible in his top pocket.

I phoned the emergency services and waited nearby to watch the results. It was some time, much to my chagrin, as I had been clear on all the details, before the corpse was carted off. Some uniforms arrived soon after and promptly cordoned the area off. I went back home and waited patiently by the phone. But there was no call. It could, relatively speaking, have been down to several factors, but the one poignant factor I realized was that the police probably considered the death suspicious and wanted an autopsy. I decided that the best way forward to speed up the whole thing was to just leave the torso next time; then the police wouldn't have to worry themselves about trying to identify the corpse and let the transplant organ harvesters get on with their task. On the next job, I decided I would take a freezer box, an apron, and a good collection of butcher knives, no matter how much it might disturb the client.

Over the next few weeks, I was lucky enough to get quite a few decent subjects one after another. Completely separating the torso was much messier work than I thought it would be. Who would have thought the human body held so much blood; also, the amount of flesh increased exponentially when it was chopped up.

Unfortunately, the torsos were ignored just as much as my first job was, and I only succeeded in terrifying half of London into believing that a mad serial killer was on the loose, inevitably nicknamed by the tabloids as "the Torso Terror."

I had disposed of all my victims' limbs in one of the Firm's furnaces designed for just such purposes. But the tabloids noted the fact that none of the limbs or the head of the victims had been found and gleefully seized on the idea that the Terror was, in fact, a cannibal. They painted vivid pictures of how he might be preparing and eating his victims. One paper even went so far as to ask readers to send in their cooking suggestions. The fuzz was also getting pretty hot, so I eased up on the dissections for a while. In the end, they arrested some poor loony who confessed to all of the crimes and quite a few others that the Old Bill hadn't managed to solve. Everyone was happy. Except me.

A month and a half had gone past, and I still hadn't got the call from the hospital. I did, however, get a call from my employers. They were pleased with the results I had been getting - never had debtors been so keen to pay off loans - but they were concerned that I might be becoming a bit over-zealous in my work. The debt money was being repaid faster than ever, so they didn't complain too much.

I decided what I really needed was a good old-fashioned disaster with plenty of near-intact corpses. A train accident or a motorway pile up would be just the job. I stopped short of wholesale mass murder. It didn't seem right, a load of innocent people dying like that; I did have some principles. Also, I did not want the already stressed NHS to become overworked and neglect the transplant side of things. Slow but steady was the way. But I knew time was inexorably running out, and if worst came to worst …

I racked my brains for days. And then I struck gold. I'd been watching an old re-run of *West Side Story* on daytime TV when it came to me—I'd start a turf war. It just shows how stressed I'd become that it hadn't occurred to me sooner. It was bound to supply plenty of corpses, moreover, corpses of people who probably deserved to be dead. I felt practically philanthropical. There was even a bonus supplied by modern technology which directly benefitted me. Lately, the gangs had been opting for headshots due to the unsporting behavior of certain cowardly criminals who insisted on wearing bulletproof vests. This, of course, nicely protected most of their vital organs, especially the one that was vital to me. I even made a point of telling my lowlife associates what a good thing vests were and that wearing one on the street should be a matter of course, plain common sense, really, a bit like putting your safety belt on or a crash helmet. In the same breath, I urged them to aim for the head and to make sure it was a kill shot. As an added incentive, I offered to get them a vest on the cheap provided they filled in the organ donation form for a "mate."

It wasn't difficult to get the gangs at each other's throats. Most of them hated each other, never mind the other gangs.

To get the ball rolling, as it were, I waited in a dark alley and beat John "the Baptist" Jacob's (so called because of his habit of torturing people in a bucket full of water) brains out with a baseball bat. It was well known that this was "Mad" Mick McCarthy's weapon of choice (he was a frustrated cricket player) and that he had a grudge against John.

It wasn't long before a full scale war broke out and London's streets were awash with the injured and dying bodies of villains, and in consequence, lots of fresh livers. By carefully and surreptitiously bumping off the odd popular villain, I managed to escalate the turf war into a full scale Armageddon between those south and north of the river. It was like the good ol' days of the Krays and Richardsons' feud all over again.

Inevitably it dragged in my own employers. They met their quietus by being force-fed their own ledger books. A brilliant innovation of sublime poetic justice. By a happy coincidence, it also meant that with the demise of my employers and their records (which no one cared to retrieve), I was no longer in debt when I did finally get my liver.

I was doubly pleased because it was obvious to me by then that my body was pre-disposed to only receive a villain's liver.

I am well.

THE POTATO PLANT

I drank the brandy down in one gulp. Several kind fellows gathered around me, patting me on the back and generally making sympathetic noises for the unpleasantness, whilst, at the same time, making every excuse possible for the steward. The waiter was newly employed at the club, it wasn't his fault, he was not to know, he had not been warned, and so on.

They droned their excuses for the poor wretch in my ear until it became positively tiresome. I suppose, all in all, it wasn't his fault, really. People who didn't know me or know of my history were naturally ill-prepared for my violent reaction to a certain root vegetable; I cannot name it. No, I cannot. So, please, do not importune me by soliciting it.

He had brought the selection of vegetables to the table perfunctorily enough. He had parked the trolley next to our table and deftly removed the lid of the silver tureen, and there amongst the carrots, peas and parsnips were potatoes...POTATOES!. Now, I have said it. Even the word turns my stomach to jelly. I usually try to refer to it by its botanical name, *Solanum tuberosum*, when I am in conversation with other people so I can keep my food down, which, as everyone acquainted with me knows, is mostly meat, and because I like it rare, it takes a fair deal of mastication.

I reacted instinctively, overturning the trolley and kicking the tureen as far away as possible and then turning on the waiter with my fork. Luckily for the waiter, my friends restrained me before things turned ugly. I had no desire to return for another extended stay at Dr. Thornton's "rest home," as the clinician's sanatorium was euphemistically known. The nerve doctor's regime could be quite strict, and what's more, the dreadful man forbade red meat, believing it to be insalubrious and detrimental to mental well-being. a load of poppycock and nonsense if there ever was.

I suppose it behooves me to introduce myself and explain my extraordinary behavior. I am the well-known explorer Major Percival Fallcett. If you haven't heard of me, that is your damned fault, and you should keep up with current affairs. I am famous for discovering the remnants of an ancient civilization and its lost city, which we shall call Y, in the upper regions of the Amazon in South America.

My present "impediment" owes its origin to a recent adventure which began as follows. (I should warn you at this point that the story I am about to relate to you may lead you to question my sanity, but I can assure you it is all completely true, a fact to which the good doctor himself will readily testify—or by God, I'll do for him).

I had been approached by the Royal Geographical Society to mount yet another expedition to the Amazon, which was to be financed by his majesty himself, King George V.

It would be my fourth expedition to South America. This time, it was to the upper reaches of the Orinoco River in Venezuela in search of the legendary lost city of El Dorado. The city I believed, in fact, to be Y. I readily agreed.

I had spent all of three, long joyful days with my loving wife and children, after being away for five years, and time was once again weighing heavy on my hands. For a man of action like myself, such indolence was suffocating

Unfortunately, there were no survivors from my previous expeditions, so it meant that the team I put together were mostly amateurs and had no experience of jungle survival. I had plenty of experience of licking young men into shape, so I was not that perturbed. But I have to say that at the time, I really had no inkling of how very little they knew of actual exploration in general until we reached Venezuela. Still, they were all hardy, brave fellows and a credit to their king and country.

The first thing that one must contend with in South America is, of course, the heat. My companions had not packed suitable clothing, and soon they were struggling through the jungle in sweat-sodden garments more suited to the pleasant English summer and not the suffocating, scorching heat and humidity of Venezuela. I had warned them that cricket jumpers would be entirely out of keeping with the weather in the Caribbean, but there had been no dissuading them. Most of the men were old Etonians or Harrovians, and summer weather meant cricket.

I was suitably comfortable with my linen garments. They were ideally suited to tropical climes, but even I found myself perspiring heavily under my pith helmet. My mule was also infernally uncomfortable, and much to my distress, I was starting to develop saddle sores, as were several of my companions. As soon as it became impossible to ride, I shot it.

The nights were the worst; once our insufferably lazy bearers and guides had set up our camp, cooked our evening three-course meal, dug our latrines, and washed our unmentionables, there was the incessant noise of the jungle to contend with. It spoilt a good many of our whist drives, which were also ruined by the state of the crusted port, which had not traveled well. We were plagued by insects and, even our scientifically proven repellents were no match for the Venezuelan bugs, although Smith did discover that the repellents worked rather better when applied to the skin rather than swallowed. The natives had some vile concoction which they rubbed on themselves, but no self-respecting white man would abide smelling worse than the animal he was riding. Besides, it is well known that the Latin American peasant has a lot thicker skin, more akin to animal hide than human, thus rendering them impervious to the biting fly and the effects of soap.

It soon became apparent after a few weeks that the ancient trail of the conquistadores which we had been following was so overgrown that we would have to leave what remained of the mules and proceed on foot. We left one of the natives to take care of them.

As we set out, now pedestrianized, I reminded my companions that the original conquistadores had forged this trail wearing heavy chain mail and suits of armor. Those men must have possessed superhuman strength and determination. And probably no sense of smell.

I looked at our bedraggled mob; it really was a pitiful sight. Unbelievably, it was the natives who looked the healthier, even though they were loaded down with all the expedition's equipment, as none of our group felt strong enough to carry anything. It was only I who had managed to carry the team's binoculars since we had arrived in South America. They had made my shoulder ache, and God knows it was uncomfortable enough riding piggy-back. The natives were proving more truculent than the mules and did not respond well to being spurred. But we got along as best we could.

Even worse, a crate of fine vintage sherry and two cases of claret had gone missing. We had been forced to drink inferior wines with our meals, and we had also had to abandon the Stilton as our guides refused to carry it, maintaining it was the devil's food and stank of Hell itself.

One of the scientists in the expedition, a mycologist of some repute, had discovered a new species of mushroom which had proved to be very tasty and had the unusual salutary effect of raising one's spirits. Its appearance belied its flavor and effects. It was not a flamboyant plant. There was none of the gaudiness, for example of the fly agaric, or as it is known in natural philosophy, *Amanita muscaria,* which also abounded in our surroundings. It was a simple brown spotted mushroom similar in many ways to our very own delicious chestnut mushroom. Such was its very plainness that it could not help but catch the eye given its exotic neighbors. The effects of this mushroom were similar to a mild and pleasant intoxication. However, our bearers regarded the mushroom with horror and admonished us for feasting on it, as they maintained it was inhabited by evil spirits. The leader of our guides, Juan Mata, warned against eating too many of them, saying that in large doses, they were hallucinogenic, but of course, this was poppycock. An Englishman of good breeding stock does not suffer from hallucinations.

The jungle was getting more impenetrable by the day. We now fed exclusively off the strange meats of the rainforest which our bearers caught for us. Monkey, snakes, and spiders became our staple diet. Sadly, the delicious mushrooms seemed to have disappeared. The mulattos dried the meat into a kind of jerky so we could carry it with us. We had degenerated to eating with our hands, like the natives, as we were without our pack animals, who had carried most of our extensive dinner service.

I was an old hand and used to roughing it; however, some of the youngsters took it pretty badly, especially when, on top of all our deprivations, we had to sit on the jungle floor, as our tables and chairs had also been left behind.

We had penetrated deep into the forest and reached the ruins of some long-forgotten temple when our guides turned on us. They flatly refused to go any further. They claimed the place was cursed and that it was time to turn back. There was no talking them out of it.

We let them go with some regret as they had been very useful at carrying our necessities. As it was, we decided to set up camp there and use it as our base. I was not worried about finding our way back as we had mapped out our course carefully. As to food, the temple was covered in our favorite mushrooms. We also had a plentiful supply of jerky.

Many of the team were in a pretty weak state by now. Deprived of life's basic sustenance like afternoon tea and cucumber sandwiches, their digestive systems had been hit badly. We decided we would rest up for the necessary time it took for them to recuperate. I, however, wanted to reconnoiter the surrounding territory. The youngest and fittest of our team, Tom Feathergill, chose to accompany me.

The jungle further on from the temple was more impenetrable than any we had previously traversed, and we were constantly swinging our machetes until our arms grew numb. Then disaster struck...

We both fell simultaneously into what seemed a fathomless pit. I was the first to gain consciousness and examined my body for fractures of any kind; apart from severe bruising, scratches, a twisted ankle, and several bumps to the head, I seemed to have escaped the fall relatively unscathed. I had been lucky as I had fallen on a pile of fallen branches and leaves. Perhaps at one time, the pit had been used to trap forest animals by local tribesmen; it had been so cunningly disguised. Whatever it was, it must have fallen into disuse years ago.

In the gloom of the pit, I looked for Feathergill. He had fallen on the opposite side and was still unconscious. I judged, by the awkward angle of his right leg that, he had not been so fortunate in his landing.

I crawled over to him. Thankfully, the brave young fellow was still breathing, if somewhat laboriously. I lay down beside him, trying not to disturb the poor chap. No doubt, he would be in a lot of pain when he regained consciousness. As I rested my back on the rocky wall, I noticed it was damp. In fact, it was quite wet. The walls of the pit were sheer and high and as smooth as marble; there could be no hope of climbing out of the trap. We would have to wait for help. I was sure that when we didn't return by nightfall, our team would send out a search party the very next day. It was already starting to grow dark. Night was coming. I decided it would be best to rest, sleep if we could, and make our plans the next day. I crawled away from the damp wall and lay down on my *pro tempore* bed of twigs and leaves. I fell into a deep sleep, secure in the knowledge that the new day would bring fresh hope. I always believed in hope.

I was awakened the next day by groans of pain from Tom. I suppose my eyes had now become more accustomed to the dim light, because I could make things out much more clearly. As the sun rose, it was almost as if the pit were dimly candlelit. I crawled over to my companion.

"Have some water, dear chap," I said, gently dribbling some of the contents of my flask into his mouth.

"It hurts, Percy. I think I've done something to my leg," the staunch fellow replied between painful swallows.

"I think you may have broken it old man," I told him. This was a complete understatement, because, by the morning light, I could see that the limb was contorted in all directions. I rummaged in my rucksack for my ampoules of morphine, which I always carry on expeditions, only to find that they had been smashed in the fall; now the precious liquid, which would have temporarily relieved his suffering, was no more than a damp patch at the bottom of my rucksack. I cursed under my breath.

"Don't worry, my dear fellow, help will be at hand shortly. Even now, they will be arranging a search party for us. We'll wait for a few hours until the sun's up and start shouting for help at regular intervals. You'll see. We'll be out of here in no time." I didn't have to appear over-enthusiastic, as I sincerely believed it myself.

All he managed by way of a reply was another groan. I thought of regaling him with a story of a similar incident in the Congo when two of our expedition had fallen down a ravine, but then I remembered that by the time we retrieved their bodies, they had both died from gangrene poisoning. It probably wouldn't have cheered him up.

I hit on a good idea, though, as I remembered how we had first spotted where they were. I emptied both our rucksacks and threw them as high as I could out of the pit, hoping they would snag on one of the branches above, showing a clear marker. My first attempts were futile, but in the end, I succeeded.

At what I judged to be midday, I started to shout for help. But my voice was so weak it seemed to be swallowed by the pit itself and seemed to me as if it were little more than a hoarse whisper. I bemoaned the fact that neither of us smoked (I favored snuff), because, if we'd had matches, we could have started a small fire and sent up some kind of smoke signal. It was no use rubbing sticks together, because of the dampness of the vegetation and the pit itself. It was just a question of waiting for our rescuers.

We had some food: mule jerky and pouches of dried mushrooms. But as my eyes grew accustomed to the dimness, I saw that the very same mushrooms were growing from minute crevices in the sheer walls. We could survive for weeks if necessary, so I became more concerned about poor Tom's injury. I had examined the leg superficially, and luckily, all the fractures appeared to be internal and had not broken the skin. There was no sign of gangrene as yet. There was no guarantee, though, that if we were not rescued soon, he would be able to retain his leg.

In the evening, his spirits seemed to revive somewhat, and he managed to eat a little This reassured me, and although we had not yet been discovered, I had no doubt that our rescue was imminent. I slept soundly that night and decided I would let him have all our ration of jerky on the morrow; after all, I had managed to survive on worse food than mushrooms, and he needed the protein more than me. In fact, the mushrooms growing down the pit seemed even tastier than the ones above ground.

The next day, I tried shouting as before, but this time, my voice was notably stronger; even Tom joined in, but I told him to conserve his energy. He was still holding up well, the brave fellow, and still seemed in good spirits. What worried me now was that he said that he no longer felt any pain from his leg; it seemed it had grown numb. I deemed this was not a good sign.

On our third day, I noticed a strange luminosity in his eyes, but even stranger was that a small green stalk seemed to have taken root in this right ear. I tried pulling it out, but he screamed in agony as if the thing had taken root in the orifice itself. We decided to let it be, as perhaps it would wither and die of its own accord.

Several more days passed, and I must admit I was now seriously worried. Why hadn't they found us by now? I took to scraping small lines on the walls of the pit, much as a prisoner might do in solitary confinement so as not to lose track of time. Even more alarming was the thing growing out of Feathergill's ear. It now had leaves and was growing at an alarming rate. Tom, instead of being perturbed by the thing, seemed quite contented. I even once caught him out of the corner of my eye gently caressing the plant as if he were encouraging its growth. The unnatural sight discomforted me at a primal level. I noticed that there were even some buds forming in between the leaves. I tried not to let the disgust I felt show on my face.

The days seemed to drift by in a lazy haze. If it were not for the plant growing out of Tom's ear, I think I might have succumbed to a terrible boredom. We tried playing eye spy for a while, but the novelty soon wore off, as did my attempt at charades. Then we tried general quizzes, but Tom only seemed interested in talking about his damned plant. Anyone would think he was a damned gardener entering a prize marrow at the county horticultural show. The foul thing was even bearing some kind of fruit: round, globular white things that resembled small new potatoes. What was worse, there was now a fresh plant growing out of his other ear. Feathergill, who seemed to be getting merrier by the day as I became increasingly more depressed, suggested that I try eating one of the disgusting things. I decided not to talk to him for a while as he had clearly gone insane. Thank God he couldn't move. I wouldn't have put it past the fellow to crawl over to my side of the pit and shove one of the horrible things in my mouth whilst I was asleep.

Weeks passed. I must admit even I was beginning to doubt that we would be found. On top of that, I had to put up with Feathergill's constant blabbering about his wonderful plant. The now clearly insane Feathergill postulated that you should never underestimate Mother Nature's creativity and that the plant had clearly been sent by God to sustain us. As for his own sustenance, I hardly ever saw him eat anything now. He did not seem to be suffering from malnutrition, though, and apart from a slight greenish tinge to his skin, he seemed in reasonable health. Occasionally, he would lick the walls to slake his thirst, but apart from that, he did not move. He had still not given up ragging me to eat from his infernal plant.

One morning, in a fit of rage and in order to shut him up about it once and for all, I pulled one of the fruit-like things off and popped it straight in my mouth.

"There, now! Are you satisfied?" I shouted as I munched.

Much to my surprise, it slowly dawned on me that the fruit was actually quite delicious, much like a New Jersey Royal potato but with a slightly waxier consistency. I immediately wanted to eat another one as it had rekindled my appetite, but I refrained with some difficulty until I could be sure it had no deleterious effects. Tom was deliriously happy that I had tried one of the plant's fruits, and he just kept on nodding at me in encouragement as I praised its taste and general consistency.

After what I judged to be the appropriate amount of time for the "potato" to pass through my digestive system, and suffering no ill effects, I ate my fill with Tom's hearty encouragements ringing in my ears.

I must say I passed a much more peaceful night than usual. I performed my toilet in one side of the pit that also served as my latrine. I carefully wrapped my stool in a leaf and threw it out of the pit. Strangely, Tom never seemed to pass any stools, but given his already very strange condition and the fact he never complained of constipation, it did not cause me undue worry. I felt better than I had felt for ages, and I knew that the only reason could be the alien food. I crawled over to the other side of the cave where Tom was sitting. I felt very much like a hypocrite as before I had decried his potatoes as unnatural, freakish, and no doubt poisonous. Now I was ingratiating myself with Tom in the most loathsome fashion just so I could get my hands on more of his "vegetables." Tom must have known my intentions, but bless him, the grand fellow only seemed interested that I ate my fill. And eat I did. Incredibly, I ate the potatoes on one patch of his head, and after a few hours, the plant had replenished itself and was full of fresh new potatoes.

The heavy meal sent me into a dreamless sleep. Tom was awake and beckoned me over, signaling me to eat more of the fruits. He did not speak but confined himself to sign language, as if he had taken a vow of silence. I must say I was quite ravenous, and I breakfasted well on some of the larger growths and also fresh mushrooms from the wall, which I then licked to quench my thirst and wash it all down. The other plant growing out of his ear was already nearly half the size of the other one and was already budding.

"I hope you don't mind me doing this, old chap," I would say every time I carefully plucked one of the fruits. "It seems terribly impertinent and all that, eating like this from another fellow." But he would only smile benignly at me as a means of reply.

Strangely, after that, I never again saw him consume any of the potatoes himself, or eat any of the mushrooms, or even lick the wall for water. Perhaps he did it when I was asleep, or maybe the plant itself was sustaining him in some strange way. During the following weeks, plants emerged from all over Feathergill's body, and I gorged myself on their delicious and varied fruits.

It was now becoming increasingly difficult to make out that there was actually a man beneath all the foliage, and apart from a contented rustle now and then when I complimented him on a particularly splendid specimen, Tom gave no visible sign that he still belonged to the human world.

To my horror, towards the end of our sixth week of captivity, the plant or collection of plants appeared to wither and start to die. Even though he had lost a lot of leaves, I could still not make out Tom's face amongst his foliage, and I began to despair of ever seeing my friend again. Perhaps he had merely gone before, as it were. Soon it would be my turn to join this extraordinary cycle of life: become a plant, blossom, fruit and die. I checked my body for any signs of latent vegetable growth, but I appeared clear. In fact, I was reasonably healthy apart from my withered limbs, which had shrunk from lack of use and being in such cramped quarters. Nevertheless, I prepared myself for the worst.

Days went by in a green haze. I ate rotten fruit and spent my time emitting foul odors from my mouth and rear. I began to give up any hope of retaining my humanity as I grubbed for worms and maggots like some kind of raggedly clothed rodent to supplement the decaying fruit and vegetables and what was left of the mushrooms, which were out of season. But then, miracle of miracles, just when Tom appeared to be no more than a moldering heap of clothes, thin stalks, and brown leaves—we were rescued!

I can't remember much of the journey home. I seem to have slept most of the way. When I could finally make sense of my surroundings, I was told by a nurse that over two months had passed since the rescue party had found us.

A moment later I was confronted by a bearded doctor looking down at me most severely.

"And how are we feeling today, Major Fallcett?"

They were the most sensible words I had heard, it seemed, for a long time.

"I'm much better, thank you, but how is Feathergill doing? You know, without him, I would never have survived. He must be the talk of all London. Half man, half vegetable. Must be the envy of the French. What a hero!"

The doctor coughed discreetly and lowered his voice.

"Unfortunately, Major, all that remained of Mr. Feathergill were some bones, which were scattered and gnawed as if by a frenzied wild animal."

I was deeply shocked.

"Surely not. Did some horrible creature enter into his plant and eat him? Oh, if only I had known. I would have driven it away."

The doctor's expression became even more severe if that were possible.

"It is my belief Major Fallcett, that this horrible creature was, in fact, yourself. You were under the effects of an extremely hallucinogenic mushroom which is at this moment being investigated by the Quex botanical team."

I could not bear this horrible, slanderous accusation. I proceeded to explain every last detail of our expedition to the doctor, who, being merely a gown-wearer, could not understand the mysteries that lay beyond our shores and the strange and wondrous things that there abound.

"The poor fellow must have been devoured by rats," I surmised in between sobs.

"Of course." The doctor nodded somberly and walked away without taking his leave.

I spent several more months in that dreadful place until I was released due to public petition. The good king decided to knight me for heroism. I was described by the press as an inspiration to all the British for my bravery and courage against all odds.

I felt like thumbing my nose at the white-clad doctor as I left the sanatorium, but when one is a knight of the realm, one has to maintain some dignity. I was, after all, now a hero and a celebrity. I made do with showing my teeth and growling at him.

My diet now, I find, consists mostly of meat, the rarer, the better. I suppose it is down to the fact that having had to survive so long on vegetables and fruit, I can't abide the things. Mushrooms, I avoid like the plague, of course, but that dreaded vegetable - the potato - on which I survived so long, I cannot bear the presence of. Now that I have said the word, excuse me while I vomit.

THE VETERINARIAN

Her name was Kate Fisher. I knew her from school. She was in the lower sixth, a year beneath me, and easily the sexiest girl in her form, and thus the most desired by the majority of the hormone-incensed sixth-form males—including me. The only trouble was that Kate Fisher was about as cold and unapproachable as an iceberg. So, when she sauntered into my father's veterinary practice, I was naturally and immediately interested.

Every Saturday, I helped out at my father's practice for extra pocket money and experience. I wanted to become a surgeon, though operating on two-legged specimens rather than our four-legged friends, but as far as I was concerned, they would do to practice on in the meantime.

Kate had brought in a kitten to be treated for continuous vomiting and diarrhea. It was a simple case of food poisoning, which often besets the inquisitive young who are not so discriminatory as their parents. I sensed my opportunity, and I seized it. Her one soft spot, apparently, was a love of animals; all her exercise books and even her satchel and clothes were of the cute furry-mammal variety. I intended to fully exploit this weakness in my rarefied position as a veterinarian's son.

I carefully avoided mentioning it to my class-mates. I didn't want them spoiling my unlooked-for advantage by mentioning that, in fact, I had little liking for pets generally, and cats in particular. When no one could overhear our conversations, I discussed the numerous problems her unfortunate and sickly feline companion seemed plagued with. It was simply down to a poor diet and thus a low immune system; a diagnosis I naturally kept to myself.

I offered help and advice when I could and often pilfered medicines which she could otherwise ill afford as her father, a notorious skinflint, had left the responsibility of the care of her pet to her and its ensuing costs. Of course, some of the medications had the opposite of the desired effect; after all, I couldn't allow the little furry patient, and my only, if somewhat tenuous, link to Kate regaining complete health and cutting short our blossoming relationship

It wasn't long before all my unsolicited kindness paid off; I got my first kiss and then, shortly after that, my first feel. Only tops, though, but I was pretty sure it wouldn't be long before it was stinky fingers. It wasn't all just tongue-wrestling and groping, though. We talked a lot, and not just about animals. I mean, we really communicated. There was a lot more to Kate than her world-weary goth appearance suggested. I usually found goths banal and depressing—a dying trend (forgive the pun). She was really deep. Know what I mean?

Kate could expand the micro in an everyday conversation into the macro and vice versa; nothing much shocked her. This worried me sometimes. It was as if she had seen and experienced things far beyond her years and that were well beyond my own limited sphere of experience. Things that I knew were somehow wrong. Wrong adult things.

She had lived alone with her father since her mother had died some years back under slightly mysterious circumstances involving a loose carpet rail. A loose carpet rail...I ask you? It was like something out of a pulp detective novel where the serial killer has run out of ideas. She could never talk about her mother's accident without getting angry or upset and then going into a sulk. It was rumored in the village that her mother had been a bit of a dipsomaniac, which made falling down the stairs a little more plausible. So, I learned to avoid the subject.

Her father was rarely seen, and according to Kate, he was really strict. I had met him twice, and my first impressions confirmed that. He was a tall, gaunt figure who looked like he had never smiled in his life. He had the air of a world-weary funeral director. Sometimes he would just stand there without saying a word, like he was waiting for you to die or something.

We could never make out at her house when he was about. Luckily, my parents were far more liberal and accorded us a reasonable amount of privacy. It was never enough to go all the way, though. And I was pretty sure Kate would if we had the privacy and time. I even carried a condom in my pocket, for which I had paid five times the going rate to an older boy. The wrapper had by now got so worn I could just make out a corner of the rubber itself. It always reminded me of how long I had been a virgin.

I had got to the stage of caressing her naked buttocks, although without the removal of her knickers and jeans, which meant a fair amount of hand-numbing squeezing, and I had once even got my finger inside her hole. It was wet. She had made what I supposed to be suitably agreeable moaning noises as she stroked my hard-on through my trousers. I would have had an orgasm there and then if she hadn't suddenly pushed my hand away because she heard a creak on our staircase.

Finally, our chance came when my parents had to go away to attend a relative's funeral. We had exams, so I was supposedly staying at home to study. That very evening, when Kate snuck out to my place, I at long last lost my unwanted virginity.

I had spent endless hours dreaming of the moment, but when it came, it was something of a letdown. Kate insisted on having all the lights out before she would undress even though I begged her to let me see her naked. And although she was much more the experienced one out of the two of us, and obviously knew what she was doing from the way she took charge from the start, she was surprisingly docile when it came to the actual physical act. I had to say, from the limited knowledge I had gleaned from porn magazines and such, I had expected much more of a passionate performance.

She told me I didn't need to wear a condom as I fumbled with the aging packet. Then she just lay there passively and let me use her as if she were stricken in a state of missionary martyrdom. I imagined afterwards it must have been what raping a nun felt like. She did manage a couple of moans, but whether they were of pleasure or pain, it was difficult to tell. She didn't even kiss me the whole time, not that it lasted that long anyway. After we had finished, I went to turn the light on, but she wouldn't even let me then until she had re-arranged all her clothes.

It was only when she was fully clothed again that it occurred to me that I had never seen her without a lot of clothes on. Even at school, she chose to wear long trousers and long-sleeved blouses or shirts, accompanied by pullovers or cardigans, even in the middle of summer. She was always excused from games or P.E. because of notes from her father. I suppose I had spent so long imagining her naked that I hadn't noticed the clothes.

She was uncharacteristically loving after she was fully dressed again and cuddled up to me. The smell of our sex hung heavy in the air. I decided to broach the subject.

"How come you don't like me seeing you with no clothes on? I know you've got a lovely body, so why hide it?"

I don't mind saying that what followed was so unexpected, it blew my mind. Without saying a word, she got up, put the light on, stood in the middle of the room, and slowly started to take off her clothes, starting with her top. In other circumstances, I could almost have believed I was being treated to a strip-tease. That was until I saw what Kate's clothes hid.

She pirouetted under the harsh white light so I could better observe the bruises, burns, and cuts that adorned her upper torso like some obscene undergarment. Her legs were, if anything, even worse, and her buttocks were a mass of what looked like cigarette burns. Some looked fresh.

"Who did this?" I could only ask in a whisper. But I knew the answer without having to be told. It could only be one person.

She put her clothes back on in silence. It was only when she was fully dressed again that she spoke.

"Things haven't been the same since Mum died."

She lay back down on the bed beside me, shaking in spasms.

"It's your father, isn't it?" I said.

She didn't answer but just continued to shiver. It was enough of an answer for me.

"That's why you aren't a virgin and so used to doing it—like it's nothing. It's why you're on the pill. He's been doing things to you, hasn't he? Sex things. What do they call it—sadomasochism."

"Daddy made me promise not to show anyone, and he said never to talk about it. Now I've broken my promise." With that, Kate set her mouth in a stubborn, thin line.

Suddenly I felt angry at her for letting the monster do it to her, and then I felt tremendously jealous imagining the sort of stuff he made her do, things I would be too shy to ask but would like to try, like having my thingy sucked or sticking it up her bum.

"Do you like it? Does it turn you on?" I said cruelly. I immediately regretted it. A wave of grief and shame overwhelmed me. How could I even think those things with her lying next to me in such obvious pain, a person, I realized, I loved.

She lay there without saying a word. Now I understood the submissiveness. She was so accustomed to being abused that it would seem natural that I would do it as well. I had heard about people being so traumatized that they retreated into themselves, rejecting friendship and even the minimal amount of socializing. Now I knew why she was such a loner.

I now felt sick for also having done it with her like that: in a selfish hurry to get my rocks off, using her like a piece of meat when I could have been so gentle and shown her what love was. Then the hatred and disgust I felt for her father turned to a cold anger. I would respect her father's wishes and never ask Kate about it again. I cuddled her harder and stroked her hair as she sobbed gently into my chest. That was how we drifted off to sleep.

I knew when I awoke the next day and she had gone that life was never going to be the same again. I started plotting Mr. Fisher's murder as I ate my cornflakes.

After that night, we had sex whenever the opportunity presented itself, just like normal hormone-fuelled teenagers. I had learned that foreplay didn't just involve touching a girl up. There was also psychological foreplay, being gentle and honest and doing the things she liked, and most importantly, never forcing myself on her. I even got to actually enjoy playing with her kitten. I had now restored it to full health and bought cat food for it with my own money

Kate would never talk about the things her father did to her, and I had learned not to mention it. Occasionally, when she took off a portion of her clothing in the light, I would catch a glimpse of fresh bruises or burns. And every time I saw the fresh evidence of her father's sadistic torture, I contented myself with the thoughts of what I would do to him once he was in my power. I had perfected my plan by now, and I was just waiting for the right time.

I didn't have to wait too long. Kate was away on a school field trip, and my parents were away again and would be away for the whole weekend. Perfect timing. I had been ready for weeks to put my plan into action.

I knew my way around Kate's house from the countless times she had sneaked me in when her father was at work. It was in the early hours that I made my move. I rolled a jacket around my fist and smashed in a small pane of glass in the basement door. I put my arm through and let myself in. I waited a while, carefully listening for any sign from the rooms above that I had been heard. The house was dark and silent, which I somehow found comforting knowing the impending brutality I was bringing to its sole occupant.

I pulled a balaclava hood over my head and put the large kit bag I had brought with me over in the corner of the basement. The room was full of cobwebbed junk. I used the pocket torch sparingly, mostly feeling my way up to the first floor where the bedrooms were. I had a thick knitted sock in my pocket full of small coins. It was to serve as a makeshift cosh.

I listened outside Fisher's bedroom door. Silence. I carefully turned the doorknob, easing the door open by fractions. The only noise in the house seemed to be the thumping of my own blood roaring in my ears. There was enough moonlight for me to make out the huddled shape of the body under the blankets. I could see the slight rise and fall of his chest, and heard small, contented snuffling and sleeping sounds–well, all that was about to change.

I had to whack him twice with the sock to knock him out properly. The first time couldn't have been hard enough because he half tried to get out of bed and started to say, "What the fu..."

I swung the sock as hard as I could the second time and caught him right on the temple. He made a sort of sighing noise and collapsed back onto the bed. It took a while to get him down to the basement. His head thumped on every step on the way down, so I suppose he was even more unconscious by the time I had him where I wanted. I propped him up against a big old metal filing cabinet and went to work.

I secured his hands behind his back with plastic zip ties and his feet with a piece of washing line. I wound a load of brown tape around his head to cover his mouth but made sure his nostrils were clear so he could breathe. Then I turned the light on and set out my equipment that I had brought in the kit bag. There were quite a few instruments I had "borrowed" from my father's surgery, and a few I had brought from the garage: a Stanley knife, a hammer, and an acetylene torch. I also had a cheese grater, half a dozen lemons, and a couple of my father's cigars.

When I had everything suitably prepared, I injected him with a small dose of atropine and a large dose of amphetamine sulphate, the theory being that the drugs would stop him from lapsing into unconsciousness whilst I used the instruments I had brought with me on him. I didn't want him missing out on any of the fun, in particular the painful bits.

I took off the gloves I had used to break in and put on surgical ones and a mask, also from my father's surgery. I started by slicing off his pyjamas with the Stanley knife. The thought of actually touching his flesh with mine made me physically sick.

He was starting to moan a bit now; his eyes were flickering as the drugs hit home. He was coming round. This would be when most people would start screaming. That is, of course, if they didn't have their mouth sealed with sticky tape.

I showed him the cheese grater. His forehead wrinkled up. No doubt he was a trifle confused as he came round. There would be the euphoric rush of ultra-wakefulness produced by the amphetamines, counterposed with the sluggishness of being knocked unconscious, and then the strangeness of being confronted with a masked stranger brandishing a cheese grater and half a lemon. It would confuse anyone. I soon put him out of his misery, or rather put him into it, about what was going to happen. A few rubs on the shin with the grater and a quick squeeze of the lemon juice soon enlightened him. I watched in satisfaction as his eyes bulged with the pain and disbelief.

I gave him half an hour of the grater-and-lemon treatment to get his full attention. Then I set to work on his toes with a hammer. I smashed each one to a mushy pulp. Every time I hurt him seemed like a victory for Kate, and I imagined the gratitude in her eyes if she only knew. I was the hero reclaiming what should have been her years of innocence robbed by the monster at my feet.

He had fouled himself and vomited several times by now, and the basement stunk. I wished I had brought something to stuff my nose with, or at least some air freshener. As it was, I had to make do with holding my breath. This meant I panted quite a lot, which probably did nothing to detract from the idea that he was being tortured by a sadistic pervert.

He really was a mess now. I decided it was time to get to the main event. I laid the surgical instruments slowly and carefully in front of Fisher. I had helped my father perform the operation on countless animals but, of course, never on a human being.

Mr. Fisher would not have been familiar with the instruments I was using, but when I took hold of his penis in my gloved hands, I think he was left in no doubt as to their purpose. He made frantic gurgling noises in his throat as I quickly sliced through the scrotum and the base of the penis. I held the shriveled pieces of flesh before his eyes for inspection. If he hadn't been gagged, I would have stuffed them into his mouth, and I was tempted to remove the tape and do just that, but all he would do was probably scream, and I was wary of any noise. There was an inordinate amount of blood, and I guessed it wouldn't be long before he bled out.

I finished him off with the acetylene torch until the smell of burning flesh was overpowering. There was nothing recognizable of Fisher now. He was just a pile of steaming, twitching, black flesh. A black garbage bag that had at one time been a person.

I felt somehow disconnected from him as a human being now. Fisher was just something red and black giving off a horrible stink and hissing, squelching noises.

It occurred to me that I could have removed the surgical mask and let him see my face, but I had this weird idea in the back of my mind that the last person that a murdered victim sees is imprinted on their retina. I think it was from a film I saw and probably didn't have any scientific validity. Also, I recalled that throughout his ordeal, I hadn't spoken the whole time. I had just got on steadfastly with my work. I liked to think of it as a job of work. It sounded much better than torture. I felt guilty now that I hadn't told him why I was doing it. I suppose somehow I thought he might have guessed, especially with the castration and all, but by rights, I really should have given him a chance to defend himself like you would in a proper court of law, but I knew he would only plead innocence and might have even talked me out of it. So, there really wasn't much point. As far as I was concerned, I had done what I'd set out to do. I had rid the world of a rapist, pedophile, and sadist.

A chance to explain his sick actions would have been fair, but the way I figured it, he hadn't been fair to Kate, so a kangaroo court was just what he deserved. I hopped around for a bit like a kangaroo in front of his remains just to make my point. He hadn't asked her if she wanted to be raped and abused all these years.

Afterwards I wondered if it had been the death of Kate's mother, his wife, that had sparked it all off. I could have asked him. But then they say that people will admit to anything under torture, so I guess the whole subject was moot.

I was just as careful about leaving the house without any evidence of my particular presence as I had been with my preparations for illegally entering it. I had planned everything meticulously, and after all, who was going to suspect a well-adjusted sixth-former well on his way to having a successful career in medicine? Fisher had not been a well-liked man. He had plenty of enemies and probably had made a lot more after the mysterious death of his wife. I just hoped Kate would be spared too much interrogation. I thought it better that for the moment, she should not know that it had been my doing. I would tell her when the time was right. I was looking forward to that moment: the adoration in her eyes, the tears of gratitude, the kisses of adulation, well...you get the picture.

As it was, the whole thing passed off pretty well, although I was a bit upset that the police and press had decided between them they were searching for a sadomasochistic homicidal pervert with homosexual tendencies. There was the usual panic that a mad serial killer was on the loose, and of course, that died away pretty quickly when there weren't any more murders, and the panic subsided. As I mentioned, Fisher was not liked, and neither was he mourned. Life went on, and Fisher became a story to scare naughty children at night.

Kate moved to her aunt's place, which was conveniently in the neighboring town so I still got to see her on a regular basis. Kate had seemed remarkably nonplussed by the whole torture/murder event of her only remaining parent, even to me, and I knew how distant she could be and the reasons behind it. It was almost as if she had been expecting such a thing would happen all along.

Once the funeral was over, and a suitable time had passed for grieving, although I didn't know what she had to be grieving about considering that the bane of her life had been removed, we resumed our love-making.

She had gone back to insisting on having all the lights out again when we were having intercourse. I was sorely disappointed as I had been looking forward to the day when her skin would be free of blemishes and bruises and I could appreciate its full beauty.

I finally persuaded her to leave the lights on again. It was the second anniversary of our being together and so was a sort of celebration.

She got undressed slowly, and as more and more of her body was revealed, I saw the new scars, which, if anything, were worse than before.

As before, I could only query in a tremulous voice what had happened. Her reply was one I already secretly knew before she said it.

"Before it was just for Mummy, but now I have to do it for Daddy as well."

THE SCAM

Dee paid for the hour and sat down at computer terminal number three. The "3" was scrawled in felt tip on the right side of the wooden cubicle. It was one of his favorite places as it was by the window and he could look at the babes walking by, with the added bonus that they could also see him through the internet cafe's window.

Working on a computer was no longer stigmatized as the sign of a pathetic, acne-infested, socially awkward geek. It was now cool, a sign of keen intelligence, and more importantly, it was a sign of money-making intelligence, and babes liked that stuff. It wasn't the size of your dick that mattered now; it was the number of zeros in your bank account. But just to be certain he wasn't mistaken for a complete geek, Dee had his perpetual baseball cap on backwards. Everyone knew that was cool.

He was pleased to see he had quite a lot of emails in his alias box. Could it be that Jermaine's scam was actually working? Dee was always dubious about anything that Jermaine recommended doing when it came to computing. J was always going on about all these different money-making schemes and how well he was doing with them, but at the same time, he was always mooching. J seemed to live with a permanent cash flow problem, which, at any moment, was going to disappear. D was using a *genuine* Western Union template that J had sold him for fifty quid. A template, which, no doubt, J had got from Terry Cutter, or TC (Top Cat), as he liked to be known—or the whitey-teenage-hacker-pretentious git, as D liked to think of him

On top of paying for the letter template, D also had to fork out for the software that sent the letter simultaneously to thousands of email addresses, which J had, no doubt, obtained from the same source, because no matter how much he acted the expert, he didn't know that much more about hacking than D did. It was all TC. And TC had told him they weren't even properly hacking; that was way too difficult for newbies like him and J. What TC was "allowing" them to do using his stuff was called phishing.

D replied to the emails with another pre-formatted letter. Now it was just a question of waiting for the replies, getting people's details, and asking them for the thirty-five quid needed to release a large money transfer that was waiting for them care of Western Union. This unexpected windfall was down to an unbeknown free entry they had made in a European lottery when they had shopped at one of the major supermarkets (there was a large list of them which most people would have shopped in at one time or another, and the lottery did exist). D didn't care a bit about the details that people sent; the questions were there just to add authenticity. He just cared about the money they would send. And the email templates really did look the business—very official. According to J, there were loads of greedy mugs just asking to be fleeced. Once they bit, they were there for the taking. The secret lay, according to the gospel of J, in not telling the mark they had won millions, but thousands instead. Twenty-five thousand pounds, to be exact. Winning millions appeared too good to be true and made people suspicious, but twenty-five thousand was just enough to make people believe it was genuine.

J reckoned he was making a mint, but he had still taken the fifty quid off D for the templates and another thirty for the software, and he was supposed to be his best mate. But then that was J all over. Money before mates. And he'd got worse since he'd been hanging around with TC. He'd developed superior-like airs, like he was something special—a real snowflake instead of the scrub he really was.

How could a pretentious, spotty teenager like TC be such an influence on a twenty-something-year-old? It was a mystery to D; he'd never let anyone influence him. No, sir, he was his own man—a lone-wolf. Dee secretly wanted people to refer to him as the Duke after Duke Nukem. He never voiced this secret wish. If there was one thing D was more afraid of than actual work, it was ridicule from his peers.

His inbox was really quite full. He sat back, basking in the sight for a moment. He'd never had hundreds of emails before. It felt amazing. Some of them were bound to be likely punters. Disappointingly, and ironically, a lot of the emails were also scams and phishing attempts aimed at him. D was not in the mood to see the irony. He shook his head disapprovingly. It was amazing how much crap you got sent nowadays. People were sooo inconsiderate. There was even one nosey parker with a weird name who wanted to know why the domain address on the email he had received was Venezuelan. Dee couldn't very well tell him that it was because they were free domains that couldn't be traced (information gleaned from TC via J). He wrote back to this guy, who called himself—Mephisto Pheles (Weird name, D thought, like a magician or something):

Regard the mail that you sent us, I have read your mail and understood the content of your mail.

I will like to inform you that the reason why it's Venezuelan is that this is our provided domain. Kindly give up youre personal details so that we can proceed with youre transfer of youre fund. We hope to hear from you soon so we can give you our complete professional services. God bless you.

Dee hoped the grammar and spelling were alright. He still couldn't get the hang of spellcheckers, but it sounded good to him, proper businesslike. No one bothered with that shite with emails anyway. It was fast; that was the whole point of it. English had never been one of his best subjects at school, but then he hadn't been good at any of them, really. And he couldn't very well go back to one of his old teachers and ask for help. He clicked send.

He was surprised when he got a reply straight away. When he read the message, it struck him as surely as if the computer had slapped him in the face.

If you want to steal, be a man and say so.

His first reaction was a feeling of shame. It was like someone had caught him wanking or something, anyway, some disreputable, filthy, or humiliating thing. It made D feel dirty and small, like his dad used to do before he got his belt off and laid into him for whatever misdemeanor, real or imaginary, he had committed. He felt unmanned. And that made him angry. How dare this nobody man stick his nose in his, the Duke's, business. He was not someone you messed with. He wished this Mephisto Pheles guy, if that was his real name, was here right now. Then he would show him. He pounded his reply into the keyboard like he was hammering a face with his fists.

I will like to inform you that you should never in your life insult us in any means or medium my friend. Stop mailing us please. You have been warned.

He was pleased with his answer. That should shut the fucker up good and proper, scare him as well. He leaned back in his chair with the self-satisfactory air of someone having done an unpleasant job well. He could feel the anger draining out of him. But suddenly there it was—a reply, again straight away, instantaneous, in fact. It was impossible! how could someone even type that fast?

Well, WE would like to inform you, Desmond Roberts, twenty-two-year-old male black African, that WE are on your case.

National Insurance number CH 831753 B. Date of birth: 6th April 1986. Date of death: Imminent.

Dee absorbed the words with mounting panic and then watched in disbelief as the letters were overlaid by realistic flickering flames, so real that you could almost feel the heat coming off the screen. This new message read:

WE'RE COMING TO GET YOU

Underneath were a skull and crossbones with the words: R.I.P. DESMOND ROBERTS.

The message dissolved into small globules that bore an uncanny and horrible resemblance to blood. Then the computer shut itself down. D stared at it, dumbfounded, and felt the blood drain from his face. He was not only freaked out now; he was scared. Definitely scared. Brown-skid-marks-in-the-boxers scared. He looked around the internet cafe to see if anyone else had seen what had happened, and also to surreptitiously have a quick gander to see if the perpetrator was present. The few people manning the different stations all seemed blissfully unaware of the earth-moving event that had just occurred.

He studied the young girl down the row from him. She was using a mike and headphones and seemed to be having a heated exchange with someone. The spotty guy next to her looked nerdy enough to be able to pull off the technical stuff, but Dee could see on his screen that the guy was just updating some Facebook stuff. He looked behind him, and it was the same story: no obvious candidates.

His brain was still reeling as he rose unsteadily from the desk and left the internet cafe. He felt like there was a spotlight on him and his every move was being critically observed. He looked over his shoulder quickly to see if he could catch anybody giving him the once-over, but they all seemed engrossed by their screens. He waited a few moments, pretending to look in shop windows, to see if anyone followed him out.

The problem was that the internet was everywhere. That meant the person could be right here or the other side of the planet watching him through CCTV or something. How did you deal with such an invisible and all pervading enemy? It had to be someone who knew him. No one would bother with all this just over a phishing email, surely? How else would they know so much about him?

Jermaine! The bastard had set him up. He was probably in another internet cafe right now laughing his head off with Terry. D felt righteous anger rising inside him and, thankfully, replacing the uncomfortable feeling of fear. The worse thing was that they had actually managed to scare him shitless. Of course, he couldn't admit that to either of them; he would really lose face, then. He had to act really cool, or it would be all over the streets that he was a wuss. He decided he would just shrug it off and say he had guessed straight away and now he wanted his money back. That would take the smiles off their faces.

And then who should he see standing nonchalantly by a burger wagon, filling his fat boat race? The wind-up merchant himself. D marched over to him, trying to smother the anger from welling up onto his face.

"What's up, bro?"

Even before J finished speaking. D knew he had nothing to do with it. J may have been able to pull off a few stings and such, but keeping a straight face with his mates was not one of them. D's heart sank, and as it did, the space it left was once again filled with fear. Maybe he had somehow strayed upon a weird cult or something from the dark web. He had seen stuff on TV and knew what they were capable of. Now that they had his identity, they could do anything they wanted with it. They were probably framing him for murder or bank robbery that very minute. The afternoon seemed to grow very cold all of a sudden. Wispy grey clouds heralded the arrival of a chill wind accompanied by a miserable drizzle. He made some lame excuse about having some stuff to do and hurried on his way. Jermaine shrugged and turned his limited attention span back to his burger.

D still felt like someone was watching him every step he took. Didn't the UK have more CCTV cameras than any country in the world? He didn't like this. No, he didn't like this at all. It was making him paranoid like that time he'd come down from speed and thought the Old Bill were staking out the flat from inside a wheelie bin.

His natural instinct was to go home—see his mum. Confess everything. But she would go mental, and he would never hear the end of it. Of course, she would blame him and say he deserved it. And then she would start on about Jermaine and the other lowlifes, as she called his mates, that he hung out with. The nagging would go on and on, ignoring the fact that he actually might be in very real danger from some apparently homicidal maniac.

It had to be a hoax, he kept on reassuring himself. It was ridiculous. No one would really get this miffed about some stupid emails. Would they? Either way, this Pheles character had stuff on him that he could use to stitch him up. Not good news. Was the guy going to grass him up, or was he just going to scare him for a bit and then demand some money? That seemed the logical answer. But if this Pheles guy really did know all this shit about him, he would know that D was practically skint. He didn't even have a bank account. No bank would touch him with a barge pole—he had a police record for petty larceny and had narrowly escaped prison. The only appointments he had during his week were to sign on and see his probation officer.

He walked through his wind-blown estate. He needed some home comforts. Even if he didn't confess to his mum, he needed her reassuring presence. She was the only stable thing in his life.

He didn't know if it was his imagination or the lousy weather, but the estate seemed to be emptier than usual today. There weren't even any kids playing in the excuse for a play area. He could hear a fire engine in the distance. That was reassuringly normal, at least. There was always a siren of some sort wailing somewhere on the estate.

He could see the fire engine now. It was parked outside his block of flats, which was also pretty normal. They were called out once or twice a week. It was usually a false alarm, kids on a dare to set off the ancient sprinklers and smoke alarms or some old dear leaving the chip pan on and falling asleep in front of the telly. Then he saw the smoke and saw where it was coming from. He started running.

Dee's mum was standing next to an ambulance, wrapped in a blanket and her face covered in sooty stains. She was crying, and the black stains were running down her face like over-applied mascara in a heavy shower. It would have been comical, but shit, it was his mum, innit. She saw him through the crowd of gawping onlookers and reached out her arms.

"I just got back from the shops, and boom! They say I left the gas on, but I haven't had anything all day except a cuppa, and some walnut cake. Why would I have had the cooker on? I was going to have some cheese on toast when I got back and watch *Neighbours*. Got a nice bit of cheddar...Now it's all spoilt. If only your father was alive..." His mother sobbed into his shoulder. She always resurrected his father's memory when she was upset. D felt like his heart was going to break. His mum didn't deserve this. No one did.

A fireman walked over with a clipboard.
"Are you the son?" he asked. D nodded dumbly. The fireman thrust the clipboard at him.

"Get your mother to fill this out, when she's ready. She's had a bit of a shock. Tricky thing, gas—could have been a lot worse."

D got his mother to sit down on a low wall with the clipboard.

"I can't see a thing without me specs, and I need a biro."

D saw there was one at the top of the clipboard. He didn't mention it; instead, he said he would find her one, and on that pretext, he slipped his way through the crowd. His mum would be alright; she could stay at her sister's whilst the council got the place fixed up again.

He walked away with a rising sense of dread. This confirmed it now. This was serious, and he was in real trouble. That was no accident. His mum was the least absent minded person he knew. If she said she hadn't put the gas on, she hadn't. That meant someone else had. What about if he had got home first and lit up a spliff or something. D was sure it was the guy from the computer. He toyed with the idea of going to the police, but he was sure the racist gits wouldn't help him. On top of that, they might find out what he'd been doing. Anyway, it was against the unwritten code—never involve the Old Bill.

What he needed was a good mate he could confide in. Unfortunately, his best mate was Jermaine, but J would have to do. Besides, he was partly to blame for getting D in this mess in the first place with his so-called Western Union goldmine.

D picked up the pace and was soon nearing the burger bar where he had last seen J. He was so freaked-out by it all that he still had sirens ringing in his ear. It took him a while to realize it wasn't just in his ears.

There was a crowd milling around where the burger stand usually stood. Instead of the stand, there was a cordoned-off patch of blackened, smoking concrete. He saw a mutual acquaintance in amongst the crowd.

"What happened?" he asked, already dreading and yet, at the same time, half-guessing the answer. The acquaintance was looking at the back of a departing ambulance.

"I was just talking to Jermaine. He was standing right there." The friend pointed to a blackened, scorched piece of pavement.

"They say it was the gas..." he added, unwittingly echoing D's mother's words.

D didn't need to hear anymore. He moved off, edging, warily away from the crowd of onlookers as if he were a leper. If he had the money and liked the stuff, he would have got a stiff drink somewhere; as it was, neither applied.

There was only one thing for it. If he wanted to find out who was behind this he would have to meet them on their own territory—the internet. He was sure it was some kind of gang now. It had to be more than one person to have done all this, and the Web was his only means of contact.

This time, he used a different internet cafe. He tapped in his password to access his latest mailbox. And there it was—another email from Mephisto Pheles. He felt his heart thumping so hard it felt like it was going to burst through his chest. D opened the email.

Time to set your affairs in order, Desmond Roberts. You have one hour.

He steeled himself and, with trembling fingers, typed his reply.

I don't have any affairs to put in order you nonce. I travel light. It should be you setting your affairs in order man. When I catch up with you I'm gonna do you proper. Just name a time and place if you've got the bottle.

The words sounded much braver than he felt. Instinctively he glanced around the cafe to see if anyone was checking him out, but everything looked normal enough, which added to the unreal feeling of the whole situation.

And there it was. An instantaneous reply, something that still seemed impossible to D. How could they write so fast? It was nearly as fast as thought itself.

You can come in person to pay your bill. The gasworks, Hallow Lane, five o'clock. Be there.

The old gasworks. He knew the place well. When he was growing up, all the kids had known about it and avoided it. It was a place of dread. A place parents used to frighten their children as it was supposedly haunted. It had even appeared on *Britain's Most Haunted*.

It was an old red-brick Victorian building. It stood next to an immense pale green gas tank surrounded by a matching high red-brick wall. The cathedral-like tall windows were so dark they seemed to absorb light itself. And then there were all the stories of it being haunted since Victorian times. Stories of ghosts came naturally enough to a disused old building, but the gasworks also had a history of suicides, dumped bodies, and even rumors of devil worship. Even the local junkies didn't use it to shoot up in.

It was the only place the police never bothered to patrol. It wasn't necessary; no one ever went near it. There was one good thing: D now knew they were local and it wasn't some global conspiracy out to get him. Probably some rival gang jealous of his friendship with J and TC and trying to muscle in on their new scam. Perhaps it had been as good as J had built it up to be.

D checked his watch. He would have to get a move on if he was going to be there by five o'clock. He wasn't really tooled up for this kind of gig; all he had was the flick knife he kept in his sock. He didn't like going into a confrontation by himself, but there wasn't enough time to get any of the estate's posse together. The best thing would be to go and have a recon first. He could always leg it if it looked bad and then go back mob-handed. One thing he did have was a decent pair of trainers, and he was a good runner. He was going to go careful—guerrilla tactics. This Mephisto character didn't know who he was messing with. Buoyed with this new sudden sense of bravado, D hurriedly left the cafe before his mood changed.

One thing that hadn't changed was the gasworks. It was starting to get dark when D arrived, which just added to its sinister appearance. Sooty clouds scuttled overhead, and scraps of paper blew along the empty street like tumbleweed. D walked straight past the formidable wrought-iron gates until he came to a piece of mesh fencing that had been put up when they'd begun demolishing part of the site years back and never got any further. Ever since he was a kid, there had been a gap forced between the mesh fence and the wall just wide enough for a body to squeeze through. It was still there. Why would anyone bother to fix it? No one ventured there, not even the most curious of cats.

D put his head tentatively through the gap. Just the deserted piece of wasteland it had always been: clumps of weeds, grass, and the huge metal monolith of the tank. Even the air seemed empty. D squeezed the rest of his body through. He walked quickly to the back of the building. As a child, this was where they had dared each other to climb through the hole in the broken window of the downstairs toilet.

The window was still broken. Once inside, he tried to get his bearings in the deepening gloom. He listened intently. He thought he could hear voices, or was it just one voice that kept changing its tone? On the other hand, it could be rats. D shuddered; he hated rats. He moved tentatively along the corridor. He still remembered from his childhood days that the forfeit for a failed dare was to venture right inside the building alone. Now he just felt like a burglar, which, of course, technically, he was. He passed rooms that housed shadowy, bulky, nondescript items that could have been old desks or filing cabinets. One of the objects on an immense desk even looked like a computer...

He resumed his crab-like scuttle along the walls of the hall. There was some sort of light up ahead. It was a yellowish dull light, and the bulbs were hissing. Lights shouldn't hiss! Then he noticed they weren't real light bulbs; they were gas lamps fixed to the wall, and they were the source of the jaundiced half-light. The corridor led to the main hall. He stole a quick look around the corner. The place seemed to be deserted, but still there was the low, indiscernible murmur of voices.

He wished he could make out a definite word amongst the murmurs. Some of them sounded kind of familiar. Was it Latin, maybe? That was a language, wasn't it? Something in the shadows was moving. A person. A person wearing a cloak. Only a dork, or a stage magician, would wear a cloak. D felt a sense of relief build up in him and instantly forgot the fear that had gripped him earlier. Dorks he could deal with; he wasn't sure about stage magicians.

D stepped out into the main hall. He bounced backwards and forwards on the tips of his trainers, priming himself. He was going to give this guy a good seeing-to. He presumed it was a guy, anyway—probably gay, what with the cloak 'n' all. It was difficult to see under the figure's hood. If it was a bitch, it would just be plain humiliating.

The hooded figure appeared to study D for a moment, and then moved towards him. D flexed his muscles and moved his head from side to side to loosen up his neck muscles, his ritual prelude to every kick-in. He instinctively looked down to see what footwear the guy was sporting. Then he noticed, with something of a start, that the figure did not appear to have any feet; it was just hovering above the floor! All the fear returned a thousand times. His legs turned to jelly, and he could not work out how it was that they were holding him up, but they were. He also knew that he could not move them. He was rooted to the spot with fear.

The thing in the dark grey cloak drew nearer, seemingly suspended in mid-air now. A deep voice came from under the hood. It was a voice that did not belong to the daylight; it was a voice from a dank subterranean tomb.

"Kneel," it commanded.

D felt his knees give way as if they had suddenly been chopped from under him. There was no question of disobeying. His surroundings became unclear to him. He was not sure if he was even in the gasworks anymore. He seemed to be in a place outside time and space. He had been removed from terrestrial concerns into a phantasmagoric nightmare. This was the supernatural otherworld. There was no going back. No going back to a normal life again, not anymore, not ever. He wished he could vomit. Vomiting might make the Mephisto thing feel sorry for him. But he couldn't even manage that. His traitorous stomach, trembling though it was, wouldn't even permit him that small mercy.

"Mercy," intoned the creature as if reading his thoughts. "You expect mercy, mercy for this?"

The shrouded figure pulled something out of the sleeve of his cloak. It was a black scroll with golden handles.

Mephistopheles, because it was indeed he, unrolled the scroll. D could see gold lettering marching across the page as if it were a marquis on a computer screen.

"Let us review your sins, Desmond Roberts." In the grave, pedantic voice habitual to Mephistopheles, Satan's lieutenant, he began to enumerate the young man's sins as if he were reading out a particularly boring shopping list.

To be honest (a trait Mephistopheles was only fleetingly familiar with), he thought the little low-life was definitely worthy of some sort of punishment, but the miscreant was not really in his league, and Mephistopheles felt somewhat peeved. Satan could have given this job to one of the lesser demons instead of his chief lieutenant. Was there something special about this particular case that he hadn't noticed? There was nothing really serious in the list of sins. Mephistopheles had already perused them, and they were all pretty petty, the usual human failings: greed, thievery, lust, envy, pride and if stupidity had been a sin, then Desmond Roberts would have been guilty of that in spades.

As he neared pronouncing the death sentence, which was the inevitable end to a visitation from Mephistopheles, he noticed something strange about the quaking figure kneeling before him. If his eyes, which were attuned to both the mortal and the spirit world, had not deceived him, the body of the supplicant had flickered. It was just for a nanosecond, but it was enough for Mephistopheles's unnaturally acute eyesight to pick up. A holographic image? Human beings did not have the technology yet to produce such a finely detailed three-dimensional image, and definitely not enough to fool a servant of the King of Hell. Probably a lack of concentration combined with a trick of the light, Mephistopheles decided, and he continued his grim monologue. But there it was again, a distinct little jump as if Mephistopheles had blinked, and Mephistopheles did not blink. It even distracted him enough to make him falter in his speech—an unheard of thing! He was getting to the part he most enjoyed, that of eternal damnation and endless torment. He advanced towards the kneeling figure and extended a cloaked arm to petulantly poke the Desmond person. It went straight through the kneeling youth's body! The young man looked as surprised as Mephistopheles felt.

"Bloody hell, D! I told you not to move," Terry said, and he swiveled the chair around to face the kneeling figure.

"Now he's on to us!" TC spat.

"Bound to have happened some time or another," Jermaine said in a rare moment of logical reasoning. "We'll just have to play our hand early, that's all."

"What do I do?" D asked nervously.

"You might as well get up now and take the holography stuff off," TC said.

Mephistopheles watched incredulously as the figure of Desmond Roberts rose and then started to disappear piece by piece. A holographic generating suit. Why hadn't he been able to spot it? But there was magic here as well. He could smell it. One of the other demons jealous of his influence with Satan? It had to be, but which one? Beelzebub had been aloof with him of late, but then he usually was, and then there was Berith, the chief secretary. He was always plotting something. But this had to do with money, and that meant Prince Belphegor, who loved nothing more than suggesting ways to get rich quick to humans. Desmond would have been an easy subject to entrap.

"I expect you are wondering how we caught you?" said a disembodied voice from the same hidden microphone that no doubt had relayed Desmond Robert's.

Mephistopheles bridled at this fresh insult. Caught! No one "caught" Mephistopheles. He would make this upstart, whoever it was, pay. His imagination knew no limits when it came to inflicting everlasting torment, and he would think up something extra special for the owner of the mocking voice. He silently made the incantation to return to his offices in hell, there to plot his terrible revenge. Nothing happened. He tried again with more WILL. Again, useless. Not to worry. No doubt, they were using some sort of shielding spell on the place. He would just find another point of exit.

He glided forward, but it was as if he had hit a wall of solid glass and could go no further. It had only happened to him once before. That was when HE WHO COULD NOT BE NAMED had been on the crossed wood and Mephistopheles had approached to mock HIM, just to see if he could add more pain to the boy's earthly torment. After all, HIS FATHER seemed to have forsaken him at the last moment. But one of the apostles (he presumed it had been one of them, although he had never been completely certain; it could have been the witch Mary Magdalene, for that matter—he wouldn't have put it past her) had placed a shielding square of hexagrams around the crucifixion site. And no matter how hard he'd tried, he could not approach, only witness the spectacle as if through a window. It had been most vexing to his enjoyment.

He looked at the floor. There they were, glowing discreetly, one in each corner—inverse hexagrams. Instead of keeping him out, they were keeping him in!

There was deep magic involved here. He really was trapped. He did not let any panic show in his voice. After all, he *was* Mephistopheles!

"So, mortal, what now? Have you any last wishes? You know my vengeance will be nothing compared to my Master's when He comes to free me."

What should have been the most dreaded of threats, likely to make the stoutest heart quail in abject fear, was instead greeted by a loud farting noise and an adolescent giggle. No, it could not be! Surely, he had not been duped by some mortal teenager. The very idea was monstrous. He would never be able to show his face in Abaddon again. It really was too much.

"Actually, it was good ol' Luce who set up this whole thing, with a little help from yours truly, of course. Not to mention my old pal D, who actually has only just been let in on the whole charade. So, let's move on if you don't mind. You have some catching up to do. This information is as much for your befit as D's. So, listen up y'all..."

The terrible imitation of an American Deep South accent sent shudders down Mephistopheles spine. Would this torment never end?

"If you care to look over to your left, you will notice a little USB stick on the floor. Just step on it, please, and all will be revealed."

Mephistopheles stepped towards it even though he knew it was a trap. What else could he do? Every ephemeral molecule of his incorporeal being screamed, *NO!*, but he had no choice. Like it or not, he was under the hideous teenager's command. As he grew nearer, he found himself being inexorably sucked towards the small metallic object. It was going to absorb him. He tried to scream, but he could not remember how.

One moment, the struggling cloaked figure was there, and the next, it was gone. The lights came full on—electric ones. In the middle of the room, all that remained was the USB stick and an empty grey cloak. Terry, his raw, acne-spotted face wearing a huge grin, strolled nonchalantly over to the pen, picked it up, and tossed it irreverently about in his hand.

"Last one," he said. "Now we can really get to work."

Out of the shadows stepped Jermaine, followed by a dumbstruck Dee.

"Now, Dee, I will explain," Terry said. He spread his arms wide in triumph.

D was still pretty much in a state of shock. Everything had happened so quickly and was all so bizarre that he wasn't sure what was real anymore.

It seemed but a short while ago that he had broken into this place, and now he was standing here with this freakishly precocious teenager, a resurrected Jermaine, and one of Lucifer's chief demons being tossed about in a memory stick.

The transition from hunted to hunter had taken but a moment. It was when he had glanced into one of the side rooms and noticed the furniture and wondered why it hadn't been removed. He had seen what appeared to be a computer on one of the desks, and when he had gone for a closer look, someone had grabbed him, put a hand over his mouth, and hissed into his ear,

"It's ok bro. Stay cool." It had been Jermaine's voice.

Then Terry had come out of the shadows, grinning and putting a finger to his lips. D had been too surprised to react and had just meekly followed their instructions. In whispers, they had made him take off his baseball cap and jacket and put this thin black elasticized suit on. It stretched and covered every part of his body, even his face, but the material was so thin you could still see through it. It had felt strangely comforting, like a second skin. Then Terry had made him stand in front of a computer screen, and there he could suddenly see himself! It was like he was in a computer game.

"That's called your avatar," TC breathed in his ear.

D recognized the room he was in and the corridor alongside. As he made walking movements, so did the figure on the computer screen, and he could see and hear quite clearly what was around him just as if he were physically present.

"Just do as we say," J whispered. "TC will explain everything after."

D had obediently followed their instructions, moving slowly and smoothly, right up to the moment he had inadvertently flinched when kneeling in front of

Mephistopheles. And now TC was telling him this weird techno stuff.

"You see," TC squeaked in his adolescent falsetto. "I'm not just an übercracker; I'm also a cyber-cultist. Do you know what that is, D?"

D shook his head. He didn't even know what an übercracker was. It sounded like a German punk rock band. TC went on to explain to D what cyber-occultism was. He described it as a mixture of the occult and the internet.

"The net is our connection to the magic realms. Just think about it: cyberspace, it exists, and everyone knows about it, but you can't physically touch it or feel it, but yet, at the same time, you can enter it using a non-corporeal body. In other words, it's a readymade magical kingdom. And now I have the keys. You see, on my cyber travels through the occult dimensions, I managed to make contact with Lucifer himself. Yeah, the actual Prince of Darkness, and wow, was he behind the times. He didn't even know about the internet. Imagine...It was only by chance he had been wandering about in cyberspace at all. He thought it was just another imagined human world, like dreams or the subconscious, which he can visit at will. So, we got to chatting. Yeah, chatting with Satan, man. It was dead cool. And he's really friendly like. I suppose that's his job, isn't it? Being friendly, tempting you with stuff. And that's when we sort of got to talking about his job. Evidently, the guys whacked out. I mean really knackered; there's just too many souls out there waiting to be corrupted, and him and his demons can't keep up. And now, what with the population explosion and all, it's getting worse. So, I suggested using the internet, and we started experimenting using some of his lesser demons. At first, it was a bit of a mess. A lot of the demons actually got destroyed in some of the online games. But the stronger ones survived. They don't like it much, being bossed about by a mortal but it gives Satan a rest. They're always trying to rebel on the net, but they have to do what I tell them. I command them all with just a tap of the keyboard."

TC grinned and wriggled his index finger to demonstrate. He admitted to having set D up with Satan's help, but it had been the only way to trap Mephistopheles. He would have smelt a rat if they had let D in on it and, as a result, D's actions had been anything less than spontaneous. Mephistopheles could easily tell the difference between real fear and acting—he'd had a lot of experience.

"We're gonna be the richest cyber-lords ever." Terry puffed out his pigeon chest. "I'll be the new Zuckerberg. No, fuck that, I'll have Zuckerberg sucking my dick."

J nudged D. "This is the good bit...Tell him TC."

TC continued. "The really amazing thing was that Satan has never even heard of spam. It turns out they have a really good natural firewall in hell."

TC laughed out loud at this as if it was hilarious, and so did J. D gathered it must be some kind of joke, so he followed suit, although he didn't get it. What was a firewall when it was at home, anyway?

Then, in triumphant and hushed tones, TC told D the clincher. He had explained to Satan that with just one carefully written scam, and using spam, you could tempt millions of people in one go.

Satan had been all ears.

INSIDE THE MADHOUSE

I cautiously squinted open an eye. Good. There was nobody about. I opened them fully. The room was the same as it always was: the starched white linen sheets that practically fastened me to the bed like bandages, and the standard hospital-issue bedside table.

There was something different on the table, though. Instead of the usual plastic jug and beaker, there was a cup-cake and a small plastic cup of orange squash. The cup-cake had a small candle in it. It was unlit. We weren't allowed matches in the ward. Not that there would have been much to set fire to anyway. Marble floors, iron bedsteads, and thick, barred, frosted glass windows that were never opened. I was probably the most inflammable thing in the room.

I lay there, staring at the cupcake for a time. I could hear the daily hospital noises unfolding outside the door of the room, regular as clockwork. After all these years, I knew them off by heart.

The cleaner would be in soon. I could hear the mop bucket with its squeaky wheel being dragged slowly along the corridor. The door opened. Time to shut my eyes again. From the whistling, I knew it was the young Jamaican lad. He did this floor on alternate weeks. He had only been on the ward for a few years so he was considered something of a new boy.

He had arrived after the time I had begun my silence, so he never tried to strike up a conversation. Not very many of the other staff ever did anymore, only the occasional doctor.

But in their case, I think it was probably more for their benefit than mine.

The Jamaican lad always whistled the same tune when he was in my room. At one time, I would have known the name of it (some song about sitting on a dock somewhere...), although, I did know he was whistling it off-key. Things like that would have mattered to me in the past.

He paused for a moment. I knew he was looking at my cupcake and deciding whether he should eat it or not; after all, it wasn't like the vegetable tucked tightly in the linen sheets was going to complain to anybody. But what if someone should come in whilst he was scarfing it? Was it worth losing his job over? He started whistling again, and the swishing of the wet mop recommenced—obviously, it wasn't. As he left, he whistled "Happy Birthday"; maybe he wasn't such a bad guy after all.

In this place, it's the people in white coats, the doctors and nurses, who have the keys to the main doors: the division between sanity and madness. It has always seemed to me a ridiculous decision as to who is to say on which side of the door sanity really exists.

I opened my eyes again as soon as I heard the door shut. I pulled my arm out of the sheets and tentatively reached out my hand to touch the cake, and then I quickly withdrew it again; I heard footsteps outside my door. My doctor's footsteps. I could tell by the light footfalls of her sensible shoes. It wasn't the day for her weekly visit, but she was obviously making the annual exception. Why did every doctor since I had been interned here - voluntarily, I might add - deem it necessary to remind me how old I was and how long I had been in this sanatorium slash loony bin once every year?

"Hello, Jeffrey," she said. She sat down with a sigh.

If I had felt like talking, I would have reminded her that I had never said that she could address me on first-name terms, nor had I ever invited her to sit down in my room.

She gently tapped me on the mound my feet made under the covers. I decided not to react in any way.

"Well, forty-nine today! And you've been here over nineteen years. I think that's some kind of record for a voluntary patient."

It must be by now, I thought, as she had said the same thing two years running.

"Will you be going on one of yours wanders today? It's a nice thing to do on your birthday. You can see your friends."

What friends did she mean? It had been sixteen years since I had considered anybody worth talking to, let alone associate with. Didn't she know this was the brain-deads' floor? Harmless, but nothing much up there, know what I mean? The lights were on, but nobody was home. But not me. I had simply upped stumps and moved house. The lights were off, but I was most definitely at home. And it was cosy in here. No one to disturb me. Just me and my thoughts. Thoughts which only I controlled and, therefore, made as pleasant as possible.

My doctor droned on for what must have been ten or fifteen minutes more; I don't know—I had phased out after the first few minutes. Instead, I was reconstructing a visit I had made to the National Gallery when I was fourteen. It was the first time I had seen *Two Crabs* by Van Gogh. I had been stunned. I had never realized green could be so green. Nothing like the insipid moss-colored walls of the hospital, although, I suppose, it was a suitably moldy color for its inhabitants, who were quietly rotting away within its confines.

She finally droned herself out, made her goodbyes, and left. I opened my eyes again and relaxed by staring at the cracks in the ceiling. My favorite crack resembled the silhouette of a witch. There was another one that looked like a clown blowing bubbles.

I wondered if I should eat my cupcake and drink the squash, but I liked the idea of it lasting the day through. I would probably have it after the evening meal, which would be shepherds pie, and jelly and ice cream for afters, as it was a Wednesday.

Soon it would be the medication round, but before it came, I had another visitor. It was a visitor who came now and again. He was an intern, the same as me. At one time, he might have had a pretty good physique, but the drugs and lack of exercise had turned it to wobbling flab. Still, he was the only sort of regular visitor out of the other patients who ever came to see me. I knew the sound of the flippy-floppy soft slippers he always wore. I deigned to open my eyes for him. I did not know his name, having never asked for it, but I had nicknamed him the Blob. The Blob sat himself down on the same fold-up chair that my doctor had just vacated.

The thing with the Blob is he always spoke nonsensical gobbledygook, and none of the doctors, nor even the other patients, had ever managed to decipher it. So, basically, he sat there talking to himself. Which suited me splendidly.

"Blubbeshoottamit harcrshac blooosh," he jibber-jabbered in greeting and nodded at my cake. For some unknown reason, and as there was no one else about, I decided to break my lengthy self-imposed silence and answered him. But in the same vein, of course.

"Blashbosha clooper clapperwhoo," I gibbered in reply.

The Blob seemed taken aback and not just because I had spoken. It seemed that the words had some sort of significance for him.

He became animated all of a sudden. The most excited I had ever seen him. With both chins wobbling, he exclaimed, "Bissha boossh clamaaaa kan!"

I tried out another ridiculous sentence on him.

"Koom trusha clipppa jooo," I dribbled.

His face lit up. He threw back his head and laughed uproariously. He nodded profusely at me as if he were agreeing wholeheartedly with a humorous comment.

"Kracked booma boom zong," he blathered breathlessly.

I decided to play along with this nonsensical game now that we had started it.

"Beeva loopa choopa," I chompered.

This time though he looked extremely perplexed. He stood up and made the universal sign to wait. Then he hurried out the room as fast as his blubber allowed him, like some unanchored barrage balloon caught in a strong wind.

I closed my eyes and gave myself a well-deserved inner smile. The first communication I had made with another human being in over a decade had been randomly made up, and a mad-man had appeared to understand it. Normally, about this time, I would have a little pre-lunch nap, but something told me the Blob would be back. I contented myself re-playing in my head one of Fischer and Spassky's classic chess games.

I was on Fischer's thirty-second move, which would prove to be the pivotal point for an inevitable stalemate, when the Blob came back, but this time, he wasn't alone. He was pushing before him an unwilling youth with wild, greasy hair. I had seen him, the youth, a number of times on my travels around the world—I mean ward, sorry, a Freudian slip. He always seemed to have stubble but never a beard or, for that matter, clean-shaven. I had nick-named him Syd in my head, after Syd Barrett, the founding member of Pink Floyd, because he reminded me of a picture I had seen of Barrett once in a magazine when he was younger. Strangely enough, Barrett had also supposedly suffered from mental problems and had now supposedly ballooned to the size of the Blob. Looking at the pair, you could say it was a before-and-after image of Barrett.

Syd Barrett's music spoke of a deeper sanity to me than a lot of the things I heard on the radio or television in my wanderings around the ward. The specimen in front of me did not show many symptoms of sanity, though. He stared at me wide-eyed and open-mouthed with his hands held to the side of his head. He now reminded me of the figure in Munch's painting *The Scream*.

The Blob jabbered in his weird language at him, and "Syd" jabbered back in the same lingo. Then they both turned to me as though they expected me to add something to their ravings. I was growing tired of the game by now, but it did not look like they'd be leaving unless I added my bit.

"Ganoof gabump baffaadoo," I gobbed at them.

Syd shrieked and started pulling at his hair whilst the Blob clapped his hands to his ears and rocked backwards and forwards, moaning.

Syd howled, "Bluu kravitza gump!"

He left the room, pointing at me and shaking his head. The Blob seemed to have recovered but was drooling a little from the side of his mouth. He looked mournfully at me. A single tear trickled down his cheek. Then he, too, left the room and closed the door behind him with a heavy sigh.

I pulled the bedside table closer and ate the cupcake. Then I washed it all down with the weak orange squash. I lay my head back down on the pillow and closed my eyes. That was it for another year.

THE KNOCKER

The Knocker was about. I could smell him. That peculiar stench of unwashed flesh, dried blood, piss, and sweat. In the orphanage, we had nicknamed him Stinker. And Stinker was on the prowl. It would go hard for any young lad he caught out of bed. I should sleep. I knew that.

I had a hard day's graft ahead of me, but drifting off to sleep was difficult, what with Stinker prowling about. There were also the snores and mutterings of my bed-fellows to keep me awake, as well as the constant nips from lice, which you knew, if you itched, then they would itch more; the temptation for a moment's respite was unbearable.

Yesterday had been knackering, shoveling muck from a blocked sewer, barrowing the stuff to the river, and dumping it in the yellow broth. I ached all over. But the new job the Knocker had found me promised to be something different entirely. I suppose the real reason for my unwanted somnambulism was due to excitement. I was going to do some secretarial work for some bigwig professor in town—London town.

Normally, they would never take a child from the orphanage for such a task. Most of us couldn't even make our mark, let alone read or write. But Stinker knew about my background, about my wealthy parents before the family's financial ruin and their deaths, and, of course, my private and superior education.

Since I had arrived at the orphanage, Stinker had used this knowledge as a weapon against me. He would hire me out for the most menial and demeaning work available, reveling in the disgust he knew it caused me. He must have been getting a big kickback on this job to have let his little secret out. There was a risk someone might actually want to adopt me if they found I was educated and had agreeable habits and manners. There was a shortage of children since the plague, and ones with some semblance of intelligence were particularly valued.

Stinker was close now. The smell was very nearly overpowering. I squeezed my eyes tightly shut and tried not to gag out loud. I heard his heavy breathing at the bottom of the wooden pallet I shared with three other boys. I could smell the rum and various stomach acids wafting over us like a polluted tide, the burning of a gut whose owner had ceased caring about its contents or its produce. Stinker burped and farted his way around the pallet. No wonder he was on one of his wanders; he was stinking drunk (pardon the pun).

He was probably hoping that he could find one of the smaller boys awake and coerce him back to his so-called office for his perverted and obnoxious pleasure. Many a young boy began a life of sodomy and abuse in that cramped and stinking hole when Stinker had the rum on him. I could feel the thin blanket moving as he unsuccessfully tried to touch the boys' rumps. We had learned to sleep on our backs. Woe betide a boy sleeping on his side or on his face; he would be awoken by the unceremonious insertion of Stinker's rough finger in his hole. I heard him stagger away, muttering to himself. No doubt he was going back to the office to console himself with his bottle. It would be safe to sleep for a while. I found myself drifting off.

We were woken, as usual, by the dreadful shrieking of the new boys being thrashed out of their beds with a switch and made to stand on the freezing cobblestones whilst Stinker made the rounds with a bucket of scummy water and a filthy rag with which he rubbed their faces red raw. He would treat them rougher when he carried a hangover.

We trudged to the dining hall for our daily bowl of cold lumped porridge and slice of stale bread. My stomach rumbled in expectation. It was a wonder anyone could feel hunger for such unappetizing fare. This was supposed to maintain us for the day. We were expected to supplement our diet by begging the public for scraps. We had all perfected the hungry hangdog look that provided the charity; anything else we were given went Stinker's way. Nothing got past him. He regularly checked us over with his greasy mitts in case we had hidden anything of value, and he helped himself to a sly grope the meanwhile.

Stinker yanked me out of the hall before I had time to wipe my bowl clean with my last morsel of bread.

"Come on, you lazy lout. Can't be late on your first day."

He was called the "Knocker" because that's what he did—he knocked. He knocked on people's doors and found jobs for us poor little orphans. "God's forgotten little angels," he called us when he made his spiel. He employed us to the public for a pittance on behalf of the charitable concerns of the orphanage, but what he neglected to mention to our charitable employers, known to us as the "Gobblers" on account of the amount of food they stuffed in their fat maws, was that a good part of that pittance went in his pocket and not the coffers of the orphanage.

We drew up outside a suitably impressive house. I jumped off the back of the cart before Stinker could lay his horrible mitts on me. He rapped on the huge door with his cudgel-come-log he called his "Knobbler." It was opened by a butler! I hadn't seen one since the death of my parents. I wondered how the people who lived here even let someone like Stinker cross the threshold; the butler seemed to share my impression. We were told to wait in the entrance hall. Presently a very dapper old man with huge whiskers, wearing a maroon velvet smoking jacket and cap, appeared before us.

"Welcome, welcome," he said cheerfully, clapping his hands and giving me a friendly pat on the head. I noticed he didn't even recoil at the greasy mess of my hair and the vermin that inhabited it.

"So this is the young lad. Splendid, splendid," he said. I had already noticed that one of his idiosyncrasies was to repeat certain words when he was excited or happy.

He slipped the Knocker a coin and dismissed him with a wave of the hand. Stinker slunk off with a horrible leer in my direction whilst bowing and scraping his way out the door.

"Come, come, my boy."

I followed the kindly gentleman down some steps and into a brightly lit chamber.

"Behold, young man—my laboratory."

He nodded and waved his arm around the huge room as if it needed an introduction. I had never seen so much gleaming machinery in one place, and there in a corner, dominating the whole room with its lordly presence—it stood.

I had never seen one before, but I knew what it was before the ancient even spoke its name.

"And that's my thinking machine, or arithmometer, as some people call them."

His eyes sparkled with pride.

"I'm Professor Mitchell, but you may call me Mitch. All my friends do, and I hope we will be friends."

I was speechless. I had never been spoken to or treated by an adult in this manner before, even in my precocious youth. I had prepared myself and was half-expecting at least a small beating before starting whatever work had been allotted me. Then the Professor, I still could not bring myself to think of him as Mitch, went to a speaking tube set in the wall and, without further ado ordered milk and biscuits.

"First things first," he said, rubbing his hands together, which I was to learn was also another habit with him when he was excited.

"Boys are always hungry. You'll have your snack first. Then we'll get down to work."

A snack for me! I was on the verge of fainting in disbelief. Was I still asleep and dreaming? It was the only thing that would have made any sense that morning.

No sooner had he finished speaking than the butler arrived carrying a tray of the aforementioned snack of biscuits and milk. The Professor made me sit down to eat—another unexpected luxury. It took me less than a minute to devour the lot. Afterwards, I felt somewhat ashamed of my exhibition of gluttony, but the Professor seemed positively delighted.

My work for today, the Professor explained, would consist solely of cleaning the equipment. Children had small hands and fingers that could reach into the most intricate parts of the machinery. It transpired that it had been a task that his wife had lovingly performed for many years, but she had recently passed away.

"May I offer my sincerest condolences, sir," I said politely.

The Professor gave me a strange look and patted me on the head. He walked over to a blackboard and chalked up some equations that I recognized from my schooldays. He left them all unfinished. He silently handed me the piece of chalk. I finished the equations. The Professor led me to a stool, placed his hands on my shoulders and sat me down.

"I think it's time we had a little chat," he said.

For the first time, somebody had asked me about my life before the orphanage—somebody actually cared. From that day on, I loved the Professor. He said I reminded him of a boy in a story he had read by a certain Charlie Dickinson. The boy's name had been Ollie Twist. It became my nickname in the house, which shortly became my home because the Professor promptly adopted me. He also made a goodly donation to the orphanage. I had misgivings about that but did not voice them.

I had more responsibilities now, the main one being the maintenance of the hugely impressive copper and chrome colossus that was the arithmometer. In the morning, I would clean and then wind it, so it was ready for the day's work. Some days, the Professor would teach me some programming, as he called it, which was a way of giving the computer instructions on what to do. He had started me off on a language called binary, which allowed you to communicate directly with the machine, but the programming in this language was long and laborious. Then he taught me a basic language which was concentrated and much faster. In keeping with the Prof's sense of humor, he called this basic language "Basic." He told me that he had once met the great man himself, the father of all the thinking machines, Touring. Alain Touring had been one of my heroes for as long as I could remember. I asked what it was like to have met the greatest inventor and engineer of our times, the man who had single-handedly constructed the first clockwork calculator and subsequently the first arithmometer.

"What was he like?" I asked eagerly.

The Professor gave me a strange little smile which I had now come to recognize as a sign that he was being secretive.

"He was very nice," he told me. "A little bit aloof at times, but a little too friendly at others, if you know what I mean."

And with that, the Prof had given me an immense wink. I did not know what the intention of the wink was, so I winked back. He gave a great roar of laughter and patted me on the knee.

"Oh, for the innocence of youth," he bellowed happily.

He went back to his experiments, chuckling all the while.

Often, in my bed at night, I would think of Stinker's fury at being left out of it all, and I'd smile to myself before falling into a dreamless and contented sleep. But I had underestimated the Knocker's vindictiveness and capacity for wickedness.

I had been living happily with the Professor for several months and had become accustomed to my new way of life. All that was about to change.

The Professor had sent me out to the local apothecary for some chemicals he was running short of. I loved running errands for the Professor. Now I could march down the familiar streets with my head held high, full of confidence. I was kitted out, head to toe like a young gentleman, as befitted my new status as a professor's assistant. My navy blue velvet jacket had a tendency to attract the unwanted attentions of the local pigeons that seemed to consider it a target for defecation.

I zigzagged hurriedly across the square, narrowly avoiding the little white packages that were launched at me with the precision of an expert bombardier, and managed to gain the sanctuary of the alleyways relatively unscathed. It was in their shadowy depths that I was grabbed by the Knocker. How many days must he have spent lurking on corners and in doorways, waiting for a chance to nab me? It must have been weeks, not days. That just shows you what a determined piece of work Stinker was. He had an accomplice with him, and between the two of them they managed to pile me into a sack. The last thing I remember was an odd smell, and then everything went black.

When I regained consciousness from the effects of what I guessed was some sort of gaseous soporific, it was to the highly undesirable smell, or rather stench, of the Knocker's office. I was the in the dark, fetid, broken atmosphere of his private room in the orphanage, securely tied and gagged. A black figure towered above me, a huge knobbed lump of wood hanging loosely from a leather thong wrapped around his wrist—I recognized the silhouette of Knobbler and the accompanying Stinker. I decided to pretend that I was still asleep until I could figure out a means of escape. Stinker was not so easily fooled.

"I know you're awake, so it's no good pretending you're still unconscious, me lad. If you want to carry on pretending, then I can introduce you to Knobbler."

He swung the great lump of wood and slapped it wetly across his palm.

"He's very good for awaking young boys who don't want to wake up. An' if he don't do the trick, I got somefin' in me trousers that'll bring tears to yer eyes. An' I don't charge for the pleasure eiffirrr."

I opened my eyes fully and concentrated as much malevolence into my stare as I could muster.

"Aaah, the lad wants to hurt ol' Knocker, but the lad forgets that it was ol' Knocker that got him his sweet position in the first place. But what does Knocker get in return? Nothin'. The ol' elbow, the ol' heave-ho, that's what Knocker gets."

I tried to speak but found myself gagging on the foul rag that Stinker had rammed in my mouth. Knocker leant forward and pulled some of the rag out.

"If you makes a noise, I'll whack you so hard with ol' Knobbler they'll be shoveling your brains off the floor into a bucket."

He pulled the rest of the rag out.

"What do you want, Stinker?" I managed to splutter.

"What do I want? What does ol' Stinker want? Ol' Stinker wants what's due, that's what."

He then proceeded to set out his diabolical terms. He wanted to rob the Professor, and he required my help. If I refused, he would find me again, beat me so hard as to cripple me, and then put me out on the street with his crippled crew so that I would earn the money for him that way.

Much as I hated the idea of robbing the Professor, who had treated me as if I was his own kin, I had no choice but to go along with Stinker's plans; little did I know of Stinker's true wickedness.

The robbery was planned for the coming Tuesday evening—the butler's day off. I had left the latch undone on a cellar window, just as Stinker had instructed, but he didn't do the burglary at night as he had said he would. No, Stinker and one of his unsavory mates appeared right at tea time when the Professor and I were enjoying our afternoon snack in between the Professor's work.

"My, my, this is very cosy, I must say," he said through clenched teeth. "Why don't you sit on grandpa's knee?"'

His filthy companion sniggered and obliged us with a toothless, idiotic grin.

The Professor made as if he meant to get up and confront the two thieves. I tried to warn him, but it was too late. The Knobbler, swung with real venom, caught him on the left ear, smashing his cheekbone and jaw into bloody pieces and sending his spectacles flying across the room. I tried to scream for help, but Stinker's mate grabbed me in a surprisingly quick and sinuous movement. I couldn't bear to watch as Stinker gleefully went about his task on the dear old man, because I realized then he had never meant to just rob the Professor; he had wanted to murder him all along. And of course, I would be the main suspect, and my only hope of escape and refuge would be with Stinker. I would be in his power once more, and forever after. With a horrible lucidity, I realized I had underestimated the evil intelligence of the Knocker—it had been his plan all along.

Near the end, the Professor was no more than a pile of bloodied clothes, his body mangled beyond belief and repair. When it struck, the Knobbler now made a sound like it was squishing over-ripe fruit. Stinker finally stopped when he was satisfied that there was no trace of life left in that poor flesh. Then he turned on me.

"Now, my boy, you're coming with us. We're going to leave ol' Knobbler here. She's done enough kissing for today. Oh, and what's this carved so lovingly along her handle? Why, it's the initials of some boy. Some boy who used to live in the orphanage and what did threaten to take poor ol' Stinker's head off with it. But don't you worry your sweet little head. We won't turn you in. We're your mates, and you'll be working with us now.'

I foresaw my future, a life of crime, working for the Knocker, who could threaten to turn me in whenever he felt like it, a hunted, miserable creature, existing in a world without my dear, kind Professor.

"Holler if you want, boy. The runners will come all the sooner."

He laughed as he and his mate started searching the laboratory for things to steal.

"If you promise to let me go, I'll tell you where the real valuables are," I said.

Stinker considered for a moment.

"I'll let you go after we've got them. But don't forget, I'll make sure every fizzer in the city is after you, so you better lay low, damn your bones."

I nodded.

I pointed to the huge arithmometer in the corner.

"The inner workings of that machine are diamond and gold. I can prize them out if you give me a screwdriver. I just need to get inside..."

Stinker's eyes narrowed in suspicion as I knew they would. "What? So you can swallow half the goodies without us seeing? Do you think I'm stupid, boy?"

He turned to his filthy companion. "Grimsore, give me a leg up."

His filthy accomplice helped him into the back of the machine.

"I can't see a thing. There's no diamonds here, boy, just wheels and cogs."

"You have to go further in, they're right in the middle."

I heard Stinker grunting and groaning as he heaved his bulk and flabby limbs into the most unnatural positions; an Indian fakir would have been proud of him.

"Let me show you," I said, moving forward.

As I did, I accidentally on purpose brushed the clutch lever forward, releasing the taut gears that sprang the cogs and wheels into whirring motions.

"Ooops," I said. "Butterfingers."

Stinker managed a short scream and a bit of a gurgle as he was dragged, struggling, into the workings of the giant machine. Then bits of him started spraying around the laboratory, whilst we were showered by a fountain of warm blood.

Grimsore took one wide-eyed look, went pale, and legged it up the stairs, vomiting and screaming. I continued staring until the fountain of blood subsided and the machine had ground Stinker into a pink pulp. The arithmometer seemed to give a satisfied grunt when the task was finished, or that might have just been my imagination.

One thing was for sure: I found the vermillion tones on the bright, gleaming chrome all really rather beautiful. It was what the Professor would have called a satisfactory "output."

FIFTEEN MINUTES OF FAME

"Is there anybody there?" he tried to shout, but his now ragged vocal cords reduced the question to a mere croak.

He fell back to whimpering to himself and fiddling with the handcuffs once more. It was no use, and it was even more pointless trying to tackle whatever was holding his ankles together. He couldn't decide which part of his body hurt most, his wrists, his ankles, or his head, which still ached from whatever he had been drugged with.

The darkness made it worse. He was blindfolded with something that blotted out all traces of light, but he had a horrible feeling that the room he was in was in darkness as well, which, bizarrely, made him feel more terrified.

His throat was raw from screaming for help. He had tried begging, pleading, crying, and offering everything and anything he could think of—these included all his finances, and even sexual acts if that was what his captor wanted. Most of his clothing had been removed, including his underwear, so he could only presume that the latter might very well be a possibility. He had no idea how long he had been imprisoned like this and, so far, no idea of his captor's intentions. Time seemed to have stalled in this hellish purgatory.

He had no enemies that he knew of, and this had gone way too far for a practical joke; who would bother playing one on him anyway? He had no real friends to speak of, no relatives, and his work colleagues hardly ever even spoke to him. To all intents and purposes, he was anonymous. The only social organization he belonged to was a model railway enthusiasts' club that met once a month, and he had only joined that to receive their quarterly magazine. He rarely attended the meetings; he was incredibly shy of any kind of social gathering.

He found himself devotedly pining for his railway. He had converted the whole of his loft to contain the huge railway model, complete with stations, platforms, villages, and even mountain passes, all exactly to scale and with minute elaborate details. He had made most of the elaborate details by hand. His ample stamp collection and the model railway consumed all of his free time. During his entire life, he had never knowingly hurt a fly. And now this...Why?

"Why?" He had screamed the question hundreds of times into the enveloping and all-absorbing silence.

He repeatedly tried going back over the events of the fateful day that had brought him to his present predicament, and find some sort of reason in it. But there was none. He had walked home from his office - he worked in Town Planning - and upon entering his house, he had removed his raincoat and shoes and then put on a pair of carpet slippers. He had made himself a cup of tea, just as usual, and then had gone upstairs to his model.

He had been puzzling all day over how to incorporate a working watermill into the model. As soon as he had opened the door, he had sensed something was wrong. He hadn't been able to pin it down, but he knew it was there. For a moment, he had thought one of his carefully painted station masters had been moved or a duck was missing from the village pond, but he'd had no chance to investigate further because his whole world had seemed to disintegrate before his eyes like a collapsing stage set. His head had suddenly felt ridiculously light, as if it were going to fly off from his body like a balloon. He'd felt his legs go numb, and he'd tried to grab the side of the table for balance. For one moment, he'd had a brief close-up of the miniature field of cattle and the ridiculous thought that he hadn't properly painted the udder of one of the Friesian cows.

He shivered, not just because most of his clothing had been removed and he was on hard, damp concrete, but with the certainty that something terrible was going to happen to him. He was certain he was going to die. Die at the hands of a mad person who would not let him even see his or *her* face or hear his or *her* voice because this mad person could just as easily be a woman, although he'd had even less contact with women than men, apart from his mother. The person he had been closest to in the world had been his mother. His father, on the other hand, was a grey, forbidding memory. A dark shadow cast occasionally over his childhood who would punish him with a slap across the ear for some arcane adult motive. There were rules growing up in the adult world that he had evidently trespassed and that were never fully explained to him. In the end, he had learnt that his father simply did it for pleasure. No, he had never loved his father like his mother.

He'd had a girlfriend once, too, but it had never progressed further than a furtive kiss and a grope in the back stalls of the Saturday night cinema. It was amazing to him that she had taken no interest in the perfection of his model railway. She had soon grown bored with him, and he had never really had much inclination to pursue any other females after that disheartening experience. They made him nervous, like everyone else only more so. He often wondered if he was homosexual, but he found as little desire in that direction as he did with women. So, a disgruntled, jilted ex-lover could definitely be ruled out as his would-be tormentor.

Maybe a crazed model railway enthusiast who was jealous of his creation? Were there such people? There were all kinds of maniacs in the world. It made him queasy to think of the things he had read or seen on the news. He'd tried to shut such things out of his life as much as possible, but now they wormed their way back into his mind. The handcuffs...he'd had nightmares for ages about the handcuffs and the key.

He had read a horrific article about Nicolae Ceauşescu's Romanian regime and his secret police's favorite method of executing, or if you belonged to the resistance, murdering suspects.

They would take the unfortunate prisoner down to the labyrinth of dungeons underneath their headquarters. There they would handcuff their victims to a thick chain set in the floor and make them swallow the key to the cuffs. A sharp kitchen knife was left at their feet. In front of them, on a small table and just out of reach, was a very basic bomb with an oversized ticking clock. The clock's alarm was set for two minutes, at which point, the bomb would explode. Anything made of flesh in the bomb's immediate vicinity was turned to mush. On the table was a signed pardon by no lesser a personage than the chief of police, and it was guaranteed. The alarm only needed to be switched off for the prisoner to walk free, albeit after some emergency surgery involving their entrails being put back where they belonged.

They would take bets on if the victim would carve him or herself open to get to the key or allow themselves to be blown up. It was rumored that one prisoner had actually managed to get to the key, unlock the handcuffs, and turn off the alarm clock. He had died later from trauma and loss of blood.

Evidently, according to the secret police, the whole point of the elaborate execution was that the victim would die knowing the key to their freedom was literally inside themselves. It was an effective psychological torture technique just to let prisoners think that it could well be their fate if they did not answer their questions satisfactorily.

It posed the question: did the key to their freedom lie within themselves?

He had spent many sleepless nights thinking of what it must be like to be made to swallow that key.

In what he judged must have been his first day of captivity, he had crawled around, exploring what could only be described as some sort of cell. It appeared to be approximately five meters in length and about the same in width. There was a small hole in the middle of the room towards which the floor was slightly indented, and judging from its smell, it was where he was meant to relieve himself. There was a metal door which had a solid dull sound as if it was thick. There was a small slotted hatchway built into the door, in which, twice a day, a plastic tray of food and a beaker of water with a straw were passed through.

He had to eat like an animal, on all fours, and the first day, he had knocked the beaker over, spilling its precious liquid. The resulting thirst had made him more careful now because the sustenance, both solid and liquid, was just enough to keep him alive. Every time he heard the hatch open, he scurried over like a kind of giant, Kafkaesque beetle to plead with his captor, sobbing out the words he had rehearsed in his isolated dark world, hoping for just one sign of recognition, a sign of some sort of human empathy. But the hatch would always slam remorselessly shut after the nutrition had been passed through.

He had lost all track of time. He didn't know how many days or even weeks he had been trapped here. He was certain that he was gradually going mad. His imagination was his worst enemy. It would speak to him of the agonizing and terrible torture that was sure to come as a prelude to his nightmarish death. He would find himself responding, answering himself in a kind of hurried gibberish, at once reassuring and at other times terrifying.

Sometimes, he asked himself if this forced imprisonment was not, in reality, what he truly yearned for. Sensory deprivation or something like that, they called it, didn't they? It was the removal of all stimuli, imprisonment without sin. But surely that only worked with one's consent, and he definitely would not have consented to this.

He had thought at one time some years ago that he was suffering from some kind of agoraphobia. He had even seen a doctor, who had dismissed it outright and said he just needed to get out and socialize more. Such an easy fix if you didn't suffer from it.

He remembered when he had been a teenager and had wanted, indeed yearned, to be famous. His mother had encouraged him. She, at least, had noticed his skill in model making.

It was all very well, going out and buying one of those easy self-assembly kits - any idiot could build a model from one of those - but actually building something with your bare hands and nothing but your brains and ingenuity to rely on—that was something else. His model of the Bavarian alpine village railway station of Bayerisch Eisenstein, authentically set in 1874, was perfection itself and had taken up most of his life. The train even ran by steam, and he had installed miniature gas lamps where appropriate. It would definitely have made it onto the front cover of the *Model Rail* magazine, but it would never really be the universal fame he had secretly craved when he had been younger. What had happened in the intervening years to kill off all his dreams and ambitions? Did it matter?

The reality was he didn't really care now. He realized that fame wasn't important. What really mattered was life, and it was being slowly and mercilessly drained out of him.

Sometimes he tried to stand but found the task impossible. He was either too weak or the way he was shackled made it physically too difficult. Instead, he had taken to scurrying around his prison like a rat, and he had even caught himself, on occasion, squeaking like one.

During one of the many days or nights of his imprisonment, his stomach appeared to have become upset. It was not surprising considering the noxious stuff they were feeding him, which seemed to mostly consist of a kind of stew, or at other times porridge. It resulted in a bad case of diarrhea. Even his remorseless captor seemed to notice the stench from his bowels and sloshed him down with a bucket of cold water and then roughly dried him with a coarse towel.

He took the opportunity through chattering teeth to once more beg his tormentor for mercy.

"Can't you at least tell me what I've done to you? Please, please, I don't deserve this. Please talk to me. I beg you. This is like something out of *Fifteen Minutes*..." he sobbed.

Fifteen Minutes of Fame was an immensely popular TV show which he hardly ever watched; some of the stunts they pulled were simply too sickening. The show, if it could be called that, confirmed his worse fears about human nature. In the programme the presenters would set up some sort of shocking, out-of-the-blue surprise for a poor, hapless, unsuspecting victim. It was designed to highlight their every weakness and degrade them in every way possible.

The show's producers usually picked on people that society had decided to ostracize for one reason or another; these, of course, proved popular choices. They seemed to work above the law, claiming that the victim knew all along that he was part of the spectacle, although it was quite obvious he didn't. No one would let themselves be degraded in such a fashion knowingly, would they?

Was it his imagination, or was there a slight pause in his captor's actions, an intake of breath, perhaps? But his captor remained silent as ever. After the door had been slammed shut and locked once again, he sobbed himself into some kind of sleep.

He woke to the sound of the hatch being opened. He realized he was hungry, even if it was for the muck that was served him. He didn't know if the food was any better than usual or he was simply just hungrier, but it seemed to be tastier, saltier, perhaps. The drink was wrong, though. Not water or the weak squash he was usually given, or even juice. It tasted very strange. Maybe it was poisoned. If it was, he didn't care. It dawned on him that it was not just a passing fancy; he really had given up caring. The sooner this awful ordeal was over, the better. But the taste reminded him of something. Then, incredulous, he remembered what the taste was: wine. His taste buds must have gone dead, but then he had never been much of a drinker. He had been given wine...Why on earth? His head was spinning.

Suddenly, he heard the door burst open. He realized the meaning of the wine, then. It was some sort of sacrament before his impending execution. The blindfold was ripped from his eyes. The blinding whiteness of light seared his eye sockets as if they had been burnt with a flaming torch. Added to that, was a roaring, screaming noise that filled his ears. Human screams. Some sort of mass execution.

Someone put some dark glasses on him so that his eyes could adjust more rapidly to the light. Hands were helping him to stand, but his legs seemed made of jelly. Hands led him somewhere. Evidently, his time had most assuredly come. It flashed across his mind that this must be how it felt to walk to the gallows, or any other grisly form of execution. He was overwhelmed by an empty feeling of resignation. He was mere clay in the hands of his executioners.

The screaming sounds started to take more shape and, with that, more meaning. Then, almost numbly, he realized they were screams of jubilance and not, as he had first thought, of human agony.

Someone was talking to him. They handed him something. He dimly made out the shape of a microphone.

Words that, at first, had seemed too loud and high-pitched started to cohere into sentences.

"You've done it, Nigel! You've survived one of the most grueling and cruel projects ever devised by *Fifteen Minutes of Fame*! You're a national hero, Nigel!"

He felt congratulatory pats on his back. He felt his weak arm being raised and waved for him as other people supported him on his trembling legs. The words gradually sank into his befuddled mind, and he began to make some sense of the situation.

Of course he had heard of *Fifteen Minutes of Fame*. Who hadn't? It made *Big Brother* look like a kid's tea party, he murmured into the microphone. The presenter laughed. For the first time in his life, Nigel was saying the right things. And now to think *he* had been the object of mass scrutiny, and no doubt ridicule, by millions of people who had watched every moment of his breakdown from human being into little more than an animal begging for its life. There was an immense feeling of anger and thoughts of suing were already boiling in his brain. But at the same time, there was a strange feeling of euphoria.

The people. He could make them out now. There must be thousands of them, waving and cheering *him*! He waved back, smiling weakly and shyly, almost coyly He supposed deep down inside he had secretly known it was *Fifteen Minutes*...But now he was a hero. He was famous at last.

THE CIDERMAKERS

Monsieur Pierre Delaflote and his son, Alphonse, had been making wine in the small village of Carnacé in Normandy for as long as most of the villagers could remember. It was not good wine - the heavy clay soil was not conducive to growing fine vines - but it was cheap wine, very cheap. And that's why the villagers liked it so much. It also packed a hell of a punch, another reason the villagers liked it so much.

When Monsieur Delaflote was asked how such a poor grape could produce such a heady wine, he would merely wink knowingly and say it was all in the fermentation process; it was a long-held family secret passed from father to son, he would say.

Indeed, it was a long-held secret, and a highly illegal one. The reason the Delaflote wine had such an alarming kick was a concoction of chemicals laced with just the right quantity of anti-freeze known only to Pierre and his son.

Every so often, one of them would head off many miles away in their battered old van to discreet chemists and garages and renew their stock of additives. They rarely used the same places more than once a year. In all other aspects, it was just an ordinary, very small, and slightly rundown vineyard.

Over the years, many villagers' had grown sick with ulcers or had their eyesight blighted, but it was a poor village that could not even afford its own doctor. The illnesses were usually blamed on the villagers insipid diet due to the feeble harvest reaped from the poorly drained soil, and the bad air that was brought by fogs from across the ocean. The peasant farmers were too ignorant or simply did not care enough to find out more about their ailments; to them, it was just as much a part of village life as the Sunday church service, in which, incidentally, the Delaflote wine was used in the Communion.

Pierre and Alphonse Delaflote lived in robust health, a sure sign to the other villagers, if it were needed, that their wine was good. The villagers would have been surprised to learn that the pair never touched the stuff themselves. They drank from their own private collection of choice wines that they purchased surreptitiously when they replenished their stock of toxic chemicals, and as always far away from the village itself.

Life and death would no doubt have carried on its inexorable cycle in the tranquil village, until the Delaflotes had added to its many obituaries, but for an unfortunate incident.

Monsieur Delaflote, while straining to reach a high shelf in order to retrieve a bottle of wine from their private stock, pulled his back so badly that it left him incapacitated for at least a month. And it was an important month, the most important month of the year as far as they were concerned. It was when they harvested their meager crop of grapes and pressed them, added the special ingredients to the must, and let the fermentation process begin. It meant they would have to bring in some hired help; they would also have to keep that individual well away from the chemical side of things. They hired a certain Jean, thought by many to be the village idiot, which was not saying much, really, considering that most of the villager's brains had been addled long ago by the Delaflote wine.

Jean did most of the donkey work which would have usually fallen to Alphonse, while it was the latter, because his father was bedridden, who mixed the ingredients of the secret formula down in the cellar. He had watched his father perform the delicate operation countless times. Pierre had drilled into him how exact he should be with the measurements. Add too little of a certain compound, and it would have scant or practically no effect at all, too much, and the results could literally be fatal. The trouble with Alphonse was that, although, in some respects, he had a perfectly good long-term memory, his short-term memory was exceptionally poor, and he tended to be somewhat clumsy.

It was while turning to move one of the empty vats that he managed to knock over a nearly full anti-freeze container into just one single barrel. He returned to the work bench and righted the upended plastic container. After weighing its contents, he convinced himself that it must have been nearly empty when he knocked it over. He shrugged and decided that no harm could have been done; after all, it was only one barrel. Within five minutes, he had already forgotten the incident.

A year or so later, the contaminated batch was sold in the village market. The locals never questioned how the Delaflotes managed to ferment their wine so quickly. As far as they were concerned, as soon as it was in a bottle, it was ready to drink; besides, the Delaflotes never labeled their bottles.

The next day, the deaths started: four in the afternoon and then another three in the evening. The day after that was even worse. The coroner from a nearby town was sent for. The Delaflotes realized the game was up, but old Pierre Delaflote still had a trick up his sleeve.

Jean was still working for them. It was a small matter to get him to drink a whole bottle of the deadly wine in one go in a fake celebration while they surreptitiously drank from their own supply. Jean liked his wine.

Once he had collapsed on the floor, they deliberately cut themselves across the palms of their hands and smeared blood around the cellar and on a gasket mallet. They placed the mallet in Jean's jacket and a dirty spade nearby.

Jean would be found dead, and it would be presumed that the Delaflotes had discovered that he had been responsible for poisoning the villagers and that Jean had murdered them and then buried them somewhere in the woods. Jean had then realized that there was no escape from his heinous crimes and had committed suicide by drinking his own deadly concoction. A scribbled confession in Jean's semi-illiterate hand explained all. When it came to the local gendarme, it would be an open-and-shut case—just the way they liked them. They would not search for bodies for long.

The Delaflotes hurriedly packed a few belongings, collected all their francs from a secret hiding place (Pierre did not trust banks), and got themselves smuggled across the channel to that land of miasmas and inedible food: England.

They lay low for months, posing as tourists. They traveled the length and breadth of the country, and they never stayed in one place for more than a few days. They gradually exchanged their hoard of francs for pounds. The region Monsieur Delaflote liked the most during their travels was Kent. The countryside reminded him of his beloved

Normandy. He decided they should settle there. He told his son they would go back into business.

"But you can't grow vines here! The soil is worse than it was in Carnacé," Alphonse protested. "Besides, the English don't drink wine. They only drink their awful warm beer."

"And cider," his father corrected him. "We will buy a small orchard and make the rough cider they call scrumpy here, using our own special methods." He winked at his son, who responded with a snaggle-toothed grin.

They purchased a small Golden Russet apple orchard with its own cottage. Pierre's great-grandfather had been an apple farmer and cider-maker, so the old man was familiar with how it was done. The locals, however, were not prepared for the Delaflotes' own unique version of scrumpy cider. It soon became as famous for its potency as it had back in their own village, but Pierre Delaflote was a wily old fox, and he did not want to draw too much attention to their activities, especially after their lucky escape. They made a limited amount and kept to that amount even though they were always being approached to expand. They never drew too much attention to themselves and were thought to be somewhat reclusive, and that was just the way the Delaflotes liked it. They lived a comfortable, quiet life, eating and drinking well and sleeping in soft, warm beds.

The locals' taste for strong, still cider gave the Delaflotes even more leeway than they had had with the Carnacé villagers when it came to the special additives. The English didn't seem to care how murky or cloudy the drink was as long as it was mind-blowing and brain-cell-blitzing. The Delaflotes, who had known some heavy drinkers in their time, were amazed at the capacity of the English for drinking so much of the stuff and their love of becoming so inebriated that they became legless, as they so succinctly put it.

The Delaflotes' cloudy, literally lethal, brew was quickly established as the most popular beverage in the local pubs. None of the villagers seemed to take too much notice of the wicked hangovers and any resulting sickness either. It all seemed to form as much a part of their weekends as the traditional Sunday roast.

Life went by as it does, and time went by as it does. Everything was *bon* until the unexpected arrival of the health inspector. He immediately took a dislike to the sanitary conditions of their microbrewery, but it was when he discovered the huge stock of anti-freeze that the Delaflotes knew they were in trouble and that drastic action would have to be taken.

All it took was a powerful blow to the back of the inspector's head. They bundled him head first into one of the vats. They added a large amount of ammonium sulphate to speed the fermentation process and sealed it. Strangely enough, it proved to be one of their most popular brews the following year. Pierre cheekily named it "An Inspector Calls," after a popular play that was performed by the local amateur dramatic society that Christmas.

The Kent constabulary could make nothing of the disappearance of the health inspector. He had an unfortunate habit of purposefully making random, surprise visits and not inform other members of the staff in case they might have a friend in the trade they could forewarn. It turned out that no one knew he had been planning a visit to the Delaflotes that day. The police concentrated most of their suspicions on the foreign restaurants in the area because, as they were run by foreigners, they were by their very nature suspicious. After a few years, it became a missing person's file.

Years went by without incident. The scrumpy carried on selling, and the Delaflotes carried on with their quiet and secret criminal life. But it was to be disturbed yet again, this time by a French coach tour doing the rounds of the Kent countryside. A certain Reynard La Croix, a baker from the village of Carnacé, was, unfortunately for the Delaflotes, amongst the French tourists.

The baker decided to take a stroll by himself around the village, and it wasn't long before he reached the outskirts of the apple orchard. It wasn't the orchard that attracted him, though. His nostrils had picked up the unmistakable rich aroma of Normandy cooking emanating from a small cottage at the orchard's entrance. By sheer coincidence, Pierre Delaflote had chosen that particular day to cook one of his favorite dishes: *tripes à la mode de Caen* (tripe cooked in cider and calvados), which coincidentally also happened to be one of Reynard La Croix's favorite dishes as well. He could not help himself, and without realizing it, he made his way, as if he were sleepwalking, towards the source of the delicious smell.

The knock on the door startled Pierre as Alphonse had his own key, and they seldom had visitors. He was even more surprised when he opened the door and saw the large, plump figure of Reynard La Croix. They recognized each other immediately; both stood there ridiculously gawping at each other, open-mouthed, like a pair of guppy fish. Pierre felt faint; he swayed this way and that like an underwater plant caught in a cross-current. Reynard stepped forward and embraced him like a long-lost friend, although they had hardly known each other in Carnacé. He kissed him enthusiastically, the French way, on both cheeks.

"I knew you must still be alive. Didn't you know that monster Jean killed himself? You have nothing to fear from him anymore. That maniac can't get to you. Is Alphonse alive and here as well? There was blood...The gendarmes searched everywhere for you two. We all thought he had buried you both somewhere, but no one could find you. And here you are alive and well. No need to hide from that homicidal maniac anymore. The village has never been the same without your wonderful wine."

He gave Pierre a lewd wink and dug him good-naturedly in the ribs with one of his huge, doughy elbows.

"I could tell there was a real honest-to-goodness comrade from Normandy cooking up some decent supper instead of the terrible stuff the English try to poison us with. Do you know they served me a steak that was so over cooked I could have used it for the sole of my boot..."

Reynard babbled on, unable to contain his excitement, but Pierre could see that the light was beginning to dawn in the baker's eyes. Their departure had no doubt led to a sudden rise in good health amongst the villagers especially those previously addicted to the Delaflotes' wine. Pierre was prepared. He had surreptitiously slipped one of his long, thin, and razor-sharp kitchen knives behind his back.

There was a lot of blood. The baker had been a big, flabby man. It had been like gutting a fatted pig, and he had squealed just like one. Luckily, the farm was too far from the village to hear his terrible grunts, groans, and finally resigned sobs as the knife entered his podgy belly again and again.

It took Pierre and Alphonse hours to scrub the floor and kitchen surfaces clean of the carnage. Pierre, who had always been lean and wiry, used the baker's huge, cream-fed corpse as an example to Alphonse of the perils of eating too much cake. He shook his head sadly as he lectured Alphonse, who had a particularly sweet tooth.

"The man was a heart attack waiting to happen. Gluttony, sheer gluttony! If only people would learn to respect their bodies and take more care of them." He gave the corpse a kick.

They disposed of the hastily butchered corpse in a deep lake some miles away by wrapping it securely in thick plastic and weighing it down with large rocks. The coach party could not understand what had happened to their erstwhile companion.

The Delaflotes were on tenterhooks for weeks until the police declared it another missing person case. It was a well-known fact that all Frenchmen were sex maniacs, and an unspoken conclusion was reached that La Croix had run off with some young floozy rather than return to his marriage bed like a respectable, albeit sexually repressed, gentleman of the British persuasion.

As soon as things had calmed down a bit in the village, Pierre Delaflote complained of being too ill to work the apple farm anymore, and they put the orchard and their home up for sale at a very reasonable price. It sold quickly as the locals thought the apples were somehow special because of the miraculously strong cider they produced.

The Delaflotes found a new orchard and farmhouse in Somerset and moved all their equipment there. It was far from prying eyes and was not considered a very good property because the adjacent fields were untended and infested with mice and the farm's barn with rats. Just what the Delaflotes were looking for.

The yield from the apple orchard was poor, but of course, this did not worry the Delaflotes; they had ways of making their own improvements. The Delaflotes procured two good cats, or ratters, as the locals called them, who were justly famous rat and mice catchers, to rid the farm of its plague of vermin. Pierre and Alphonse grew so fond of the cats that they spoiled them tremendously with all manner of delicious tidbits, with the unforeseen result that they were too well fed to consume their catches, so the cats merely hunted for their own predatory, feline pleasure. The murderous pair left a terrible trail of rodenticide behind them—so many rats, in fact, that the Delaflotes were constantly having to dispose of the rotting corpses, many of which they could only locate when they began to stink, and rat corpses were an olfactory nightmare. Pierre and Alphonse were constantly filling plastic bags with the rotting corpses prior to the tedious business of either burying them or burning them. So much work for such little bodies, Pierre thought, as he followed his nose to yet another decomposing victim's furry corpse. He swore under his breath as he picked it up carefully with his rubber glove. It was bloated with putrefying gases, and he didn't want the body to burst and disgorge its disgusting entrails and nauseating stink. Then, for some reason, he suddenly remembered the health inspector back in Kent and how well that particular batch of scrumpy was received by the villagers. Without stopping to think too much about it, he emptied the whole loathsome contents of the bag into one of the smaller vats. He would see how the rats would do.

Pierre had always loved to experiment; even as a child, he had very nearly fatally poisoned his parents on more than one occasion with the extractions of certain plants like henbane and thorn apple.

He told Alphonse about his idea, and Alphonse, in turn, had a brilliant idea of his own: they would train their homicidal cats to bring their dead catches directly to the pressing room by giving them treats each time they did so.

"You can train any animal if you want and have a good enough reason and give the animal the right incentive," he assured his father. His father acquiesced to his son's superior knowledge of animal training; Pierre preferred flora to fauna. Alphonse had once even trained a mongrel to walk on its hind legs, and with a walking stick strapped to its foreleg and other suitable accruements, it could render a passable impression of Charlie Chaplin.

Some several months later, the locals proclaimed Pierre's experimental rat vat the best brew yet—just as Pierre was sure they would. The connoisseurs amongst them declared it had depth, and even a slight feculent tang, which lingered like a trapped fart in tight underwear and gave it its unmistakable character.

It became one of the new ingredients in the Delaflotes' idiosyncratic cider recipe, and they found they didn't need nearly half as much of their other special ingredients.

On a certain fine morning, one of the sanguinary cats brought in an especially large and fat specimen, which Pierre tossed over his shoulder into a nearby vat without even a glance.

Turning to his son, he said,

"You know the really great thing, Alphonse? No one ever misses rats."

ZED

The Zeta commando unit moved slowly and cautiously through the jungle, not just because the terrain was difficult, but because they were wary. Some were even frightened, although none of them would admit to it.

The Zetas are the most feared and dangerous drug cartel in Mexico, although, looking at the disconcerted faces of some of the gangsters in our unit, you wouldn't have believed it.

The Zetas broke away from the Gulf Cartel in 2010 and formed their own cartel. They quickly established themselves because they were more brutal and merciless than any of the other newly formed cartels operating in Mexico at the start of the new millennium, and that was saying something. The cartel was mainly made up of mercenaries, ex-soldiers, police, and Kaibils (the notoriously sadistic special forces of the Guatemalan military).

So, you may be wondering what I was doing there. After all, I don't exactly fit the stereotype of a Rambo-esque, macho, killing-machine mercenary. That's because I'm not, nor were the two American men in their designer jungle gear; clothes which were more conspicuous and cumbersome than practical. I usually worked as an interpreter/negotiator/middleman (you choose) for an Italian organization that, for various reasons, I do not feel obliged to reveal, but I will anyway because they are little known outside of Italy. They are known as the *'Ndrangheta* (don't worry a lot of Italians have trouble pronouncing it as well). Anyway, for whatever miscellaneous (and, as you have no doubt rightly guessed, criminal) reasons we were there, we were all stuck together in this miserable strip of sweltering hell deep in the jungles of Eastern Bolivia. And to be honest, although most of the Zetas were used to this sort of environment, they were not used to being hunted in it; indeed, they were the ones usually doing the hunting. But being hunted, they most assuredly were.

There was plenty of speculation circulating within the group as to the identity of our assailants or assailant, especially after we had found the first two corpses of our erstwhile comrades. They had both been flayed, but the skinning had been done while they were still alive. The Zetas knew that specific detail immediately. After all, skinning people alive was one of their hallmarks.

The unfortunate men had been found strung up by their ankles from a tree branch. Of course, those of us who had seen the movie *Predator*, and quite a few of us had, immediately started thinking of a predatory alien hunting us in the jungle. It just fit so perfectly with the opening of the film: mercenaries being hunted by an invisible and terrible foe, picked off one by one.

Opinions changed when we came across the second pair of scouts, or what was left of them. There were pieces spread out over a large area, the size of a tennis court, and no piece was much larger than an index finger. It was as though they had been put through some kind of giant wood chipper.

Then the screams in the night started, always at the same time—just after midnight. They did not seem like human screams, but they were too faint to be sure.

"*Madremonte!*" The whisper spread around the camp like a plague. The Madremonte (Mother Forest) was supposedly a mountain sprite that dwelt in the rain forests, a huge, green woman with bulging, glowing eyes who controlled the weather and caused men to lose their way in the jungle. And we had lost our way...

We had originally lost our bearings because of the strange weather. It had lasted for several days, and even though most of the mercenaries were expert orienteers, they had become lazy and had relied on their GPS systems to plot our way through the forest. The fierce winds and downpours had crashed their mobiles, and now we had no idea of where we were. None of them carried a compass or even had a map.

They said that you knew you were in Madremonte's territory because of screams and wailings in the night. Screams that did not sound like they came from human throats. And now these, too, had started.

It was difficult to know who was the most scared: the Americans or the Zetas. The Zetas fear was based on rainforest mythology, but the Americans knew nothing of Latin American legends. Their fear was different; it was logical and physical. As far as the Yanks were concerned, they were being tracked, and the person or persons following them was methodically eliminating them in the most conceivably gruesome manner possible. To them, it could only mean a rival cartel.

We all had one thing in common, though: none of us wanted to die, and definitely not like that There were various arguments breaking out amongst the Zetas concerning the best course of action. Our leader, Captain Suarez, was desperately trying to maintain some sort of discipline. The last thing he wanted was that the disparate groups that made up the Zetas, all equally lethal, should start to attack each other. An uneasy truce was reached in the end by making the simple point that if we started to kill each other, we would just make the Madremonte's, or whatever it was, job easier. Even so, the tension in the camp that evening was palpable.

We woke, in the middle of the night from nightmares, which made us realize how tenuous our grip on reality was and how easy it would be to slip into the kind of madness that only the leafy confines of the rainforest can produce. We crept back into ourselves and stared wide-eyed into the night until sleep overtook us once more, or took comfort in the sound of our comrades breathing softly in tune with the other jungle noises and waited until the light of morning came to chase away the nightmares and warm our bodies and minds and souls.

It rained. Our bodies dissolved into the earth, became mud. When the rain stopped it turned the jungle into a giant steam bath. Trees dripped sap sweat, their trunks wet to the touch. The earth leaked its sweated burgundy and brown blood, reeking of decay from deep subterranean caverns. Insects hovered, massed in lazy crowds. Our clothes clung to us like a wetted second skin.

The captain, to make faster headway, ordered us to discard everything that was heavy or superfluous, apart, that is, from our weapons, which, ironically, were the heaviest things we were carrying. We weren't just armed with any old weapons either; we each had Heckler and Koch MP5 submachine guns and Sig Sauer P226 pistols, except for the captain and I, who carried Berettas. We even had a flame-thrower and an AT-4 anti-tank missile launcher (God knows what for), and we all carried machetes the most indispensable item when in the jungle. We were better armed than an elite army unit, but we had only one aim now, and that was to make it back to base camp, wherever it was now, alive.

One of the ex-Kaibils went missing. We found him naked and covered in thousands of minute cuts. He had bled to death, cut in every conceivable place it is possible to slice a human body. The blood had been absorbed by the surrounding Earth, which squelched greedily as the captain knelt down to examine him. The dead man's mouth was stuffed with leaves.

A Zeta went berserk with the flamethrower, scorching huge swathes through the jungle, filling our lungs with the taste and smell of napalm.

"Vietnam, Vietnam," the insane mercenary yelled. He was, of course, far too young to have been involved in the aforesaid conflict. Perhaps his fevered brain was feeding off the images. Mercenaries love war films and war games. Maybe it makes their job easier, or in their fantasies, they star in a film that runs in their warped brains while hell rages around them. An inferno usually created by themselves.

He was overpowered by the other Zetas and held until the hysteria passed. He was relieved of the weapon, and the captain punctured the tank without a word. The flamethrower was left behind us. A mechanical sculpture, it stood alone in the midst of a smoking clearing of its own making—a testament to man's capacity for destruction.

We pressed on, marching single file in silence. It was only when we stopped for a short break that we realized the man bringing up the rear was missing. The captain bawled out the man who was in front of him. The man swore he could hear his compadre breathing behind him. In spite of myself, I felt the bumps rise on my skin. We couldn't shout out. We didn't want to give away our location, just in case.

It now felt like we were dead men walking. There were fourteen of us left. We camped for a while in case our missing comrade made an appearance. This was not because we felt any special loyalty to him; it was simply the fact that there was strength in numbers. We could not afford to lose any more men.

We tried making contact by radio once more. None of our mobiles, of every conceivable type and manufacture, were working. It seemed appropriate somehow that we should be resorting to the radio for salvation.

The Zetas (Zeds in English), gained their name from their first commander, Arturo Guzmán Decena, whose Federal Judicial Police radio code was "Z1," a code given to high-ranking officers in Mexican cities. That was, of course, before he decided to openly join the Gulf cartel (he had been corrupted by the narcotraffickers long before then) and indirectly became associated with some of my bosses in Italy.

I remembered Arturo; he would never have gotten his men into this kind of situation. Now, that the Zetas had decided to go solo, they'd found they lacked the expertise of some of the intrinsic parts of the Gulf cartel, and one of those was organization, which was unusual considering their military background. What they had lacked in expertise, they had made up for in barbarity, but the capacity for cruelty and barbarity did not get you very far if you were lost in a hostile and foreign jungle while being tracked by an invisible and equally cruel enemy.

The captain took me to one side. He didn't want the others to know he was asking my advice. What advice could I give him? This was his terrain, not mine. The only suggestion I made was that we march two abreast from now on. It would make the going harder, as we would have to cut more space with our machetes, but we would be able to keep an eye on the man next to us. Each pair would lead for an hour and then go to the rear.

The slow caterpillar of men wormed its way through the heavy undergrowth. After a few hours, we came across a stream and signs that *basuco* (unrefined cocaine washed and mashed ready for refining) had been made there: empty drums of kerosene, soda ash, and coca leaves had been left by the stream's bank. The drums had leaked into the stream, along with whatever other poisons they had been using to process the coca. Whatever it was, the fish didn't like it; several were floating, bloated and lifeless, on the surface.

There was no way of knowing if the men who had been doing the work belonged to the Zeta cartel or a rival one. The camp-site showed signs that it had only recently been vacated. Our plan was simple: we would follow their trail, friend or foe, keeping as well hidden as possible. Wherever they were heading, it would be back to civilization with their cargo of basuco. All we had to do was follow the trail, and two of the Zetas were expert trackers.

The idea of marching in pairs seemed such a good idea at the time until we discovered that the pair of Zetas bringing up the rear had disappeared as quickly and silently as the others. We stopped and stood around in a circle. No one wanted to take their eyes off each other just in case they, too, should suddenly mysteriously disappear.

Then the screams started. Thankfully, they were short-lived, but we recognized them for what they were; after all, we were experts in screams. These were not the usual screams of pain, a sound that the Zetas were all too familiar with. These were screams of fear. But not just ordinary fear. This was the primordial fear of death. The screams were something else, something far removed. This was fear of the supernatural, the unknown, the unbidden fear of something that has no right to exist. We all knew it, but no one voiced it. We clapped our hands to our heads, trying to shut out the awful noise, but I doubt if anything could have stopped that sound, not even the gates of Hell itself.

We were down to just a dozen men. The Americans were, quite rightly, petrified, and not just of the thing out there, but also of the Zetas, who had taken it into their heads that the Madremonte was insulted by the foreigners' presence in her jungle. There were dark mutterings behind their backs, while others did nothing to hide their hostility.

The Zetas insisted that the two Yankees bring up the rear. The Americans pleaded with the captain, but he could do little but acquiesce to the demands of the men. He didn't want a mini-revolt on his hands. The Americans turned to me. They were nearly in tears now, but I shrugged and picked up my pack.

When we camped that night, no one spoke to the Americans. They were left isolated by the group. They were being offered up for sacrifice, and they knew it. Something had taken shape in their faces, a mask as translucent as death itself.

In the morning, they were gone. Whether they had been taken as silently as the others or had decided to slink off and take their own chances in the jungle, we would never know.

Mid-morning we came across the other two missing Zetas, or rather their fly-covered torsos. They had been beheaded. The heads were rammed onto bamboo poles behind the corpses. The appalling look of terror was frozen forever on their faces as though they recognized their own incomplete bodies. Even the flies seemed to be avoiding the heads that had borne witness to the unspeakable. We moved on. Zetas never wasted time burying their dead.

Later, we found one of the smugglers. He was just lying there, stiff as a plank, oblivious to the gang of cutthroats that surrounded him. One of them gave him a tentative kick in the stomach; there was no reaction at all.

"Psychosis-induced catatonia," I said. I had seen the condition once before in Sicily.

The captain stared at me blankly.

"Paralyzed with fear..." I said for his benefit. The captain ordered the Zetas to go and stand in the shade of a nearby tree so he could be alone with me.

"What could do that to a person?" he whispered. His voice, normally calm and heavy with authority, betrayed his nervousness.

"Only something that the person is terrified of but truly believes in," I replied.

"Will he be okay?"

"It depends on your definition of okay," I said. "He could come round in an hour, a day, maybe never."

The captain shook his head sadly.

"Pity. Perhaps he could have told us what's going on."

We marched on, leaving him lying there, wide-eyed and silently waiting for the thing he most deeply feared to finally claim him.

That night, the screaming started up again. It had become clear this was not human screaming. No human or even an animal throat could issue that sound. How could we have mistaken it as such? But back then, it had been at a distance. And now it was getting closer. Even I was beginning to believe in the Madremonte, and I was the most cynical of us all. The wailings seemed to come from the trees and the earth itself. It was the pain of the rainforest that we heard in the dead of night.

When we woke in the morning, there remained only half a dozen of us. We dreaded what we would find as we set off on the tracks of the unknown drug smugglers. But none of us were prepared for what was to come.

The captain and I were in the vanguard, discussing our ever-lessening options. Now that the Americans had disappeared, he knew that I was the only witness to how he handled the situation, and whatever I reported back to our mutual superiors could either have a beneficial or decidedly unpleasant bearing on his future. He needed me alive so I could tell them that the loss of the two American fixers had not been his fault and put in a good word for him. The Zetas took a dim view of any kind of failure, and this trip did not qualify as a resounding success.

We came upon them in a clearing. It must have been the smugglers' base camp at one time. There was a kind of shed constructed from corrugated sheets of metal, tarpaulin, and odd bits of wood. In the background, there was the hum of an un-tuned radio like the sound of a frustrated wasp.

At first, we didn't understand the significance of the pile of rags in the middle of the clearing. It wasn't until we were up close that we saw it for what it really was—a giant barrow built of flesh. There were some rags scattered amongst the corpses, if you could call the remains corpses. They had been stripped of any dignity that was due to the dead. There were pieces of flesh and innards that could be identified as vaguely human. We had mistaken the multi-colored viscera and feces for clothing. There was movement in the mass. A Zeta let fly with his MP5, three rounds at two-second intervals, and the gas-ejected cartridges flew everywhere, winged harbingers of death. But the movement was caused by the mass of maggots that squirmed throughout the terrible mound. There was no radio. The hum we had heard came from the maggots' parents—giant bluebottles and corpse flies. They rose like a black cloud. A change of wind direction brought the smell to us, as well as the flies.

We ran, gagging, from the scene. We ran blindly. We ran as deaf-mutes, without thought or destination, our only aim to wipe the scene from our minds and the vomit from our throats. At last, the jungle forced me to slow down and eventually halt. I bent over double with my hands on my knees and vomited until it felt like my stomach was coming up through my throat. And then I vomited some more.

When I had finally finished voiding that vision of Hades, I realized I was completely alone. I listened carefully for any sound from the other mercenaries. There was nothing. A surreal silence permeated the forest. It was as if the jungle was holding its breath, waiting for something to happen. Something to happen to me. It was then that I saw Her. Or should it be It...I could only see her by not looking. If I looked directly where She was standing, I saw only the jungle, but just out of the corner of my eye, I could make out a huge face seemingly made from the undergrowth. It seemed that only by using peripheral vision was one was allowed to witness the unmanageable. It was definitely a woman's face, but it was also sternly masculine, an emerald face as green and deep as the jungle itself. It seemed made out of the leaves themselves and was looking at me with an alien curiosity. For some instinctive reason, call it a deep intuition, I knew there and then I had to get rid of my gun. I carefully unbelted the holster and slowly lowered it to the ground. A frown seemed to flicker across the face as if a wind had rippled across a hedge of leaves. I moved slowly and purposefully away from the weapon, still in its holster and belt, which lay like a twisted snake on the forest floor. A wind blew from nowhere, rustling the emerald leaves and, in turn, making the Madremonte's face waver and finally disappear.

I never found out what happened to the rest of the Zetas. And I never went into the jungle again. My only advice to those who did was to go in unarmed, but they would look at me as if I had lost my mind. And maybe I had. Somewhere in the depths of the Bolivian jungle, a part of my sanity had remained behind, forever avoiding a truth too terrible to face.

After getting back to Europe, I dedicated myself to my more usual occupation of eliminating my employers' competition. The Madremonte had given me some useful ideas.

THE MARTIAN GLADIATOR NAMED NUMBER 42

The cell holding the Martian gladiator was dark and silent, but hundreds of footsteps echoing overhead on the metallic flooring heralded the arrival of tourists come to see the sport. The Martian stirred, yawned, and stretched. He could hear the weak, reedy voices of Earthmen (who'd had this same sort of barbaric entertainment far back in their dark history). There were also plenty of Venusians clucking in their bird-like language, hissing gas ghosts from Saturn, wailing Ionians from Jupiter's moon, and the heavy clump and grunts of exertion from Neptuniuns in their clumsy anti-grav boots.

The Martian, whose name was unpronounceable in any of the solar languages, could also now hear the furious breathing of Big Larry (the nickname that had been given to the particularly huge and savage Klatck), courtesy of the cell's embedded speakers. The promoters of the evening's entertainment wanted to make sure that even the terrifying sound of the Klatck's breaths should not be lost on the Martian.

Big Larry was a favorite with the crowd and the tipsters. The sound of its breathing was being piped into the cell by the sadistic guards. It sounded like a tornado whipping itself up into a self-righteous solar storm because its breakfast had been cold.

The Klatck was the Martian's opponent in the Games and was considered one of the choice matches. Nothing much was known about the Martian, but Big Larry had made hundreds of bloody kills. It should provide the necessary gory kick-start to the Games, which, up until then, had been rather flat. The crowd was restless. It wanted a complete rending of a body, where shreds would be the only visible reminder of what had been. Mouths and similar orifices were already wet in anticipation of the Martian's cries of agony (although no one was quite sure they had heard a Martian weep) as it was slowly dismembered and mashed to a pulp. Big Larry knew how to play to the crowd. The Klatck would provide the goods. Larry had made hundreds of brutal kills and was undefeated in the galaxy.

Ordinary Klatcks were fearsome enough creatures/monsters, but evidently, just the sight of Big Larry left any galactic being paralyzed with fear. Even amongst the outlandish race of Klatcks, he was considered something of an abomination. The tourists would no doubt have been surprised, and those who had placed bets would have been mortified, had they known that the Martian (known simply as number 42) was sitting calmly on the side of his bunk and serenely looking forward to the encounter.

Martian stormtroopers were cloned genetically from a special DNA base that the Martians held in one of their top-secret labs. They did not believe in surrender and always fought to the death, so it was unusual to capture one alive. Before him, only 41 had ever been caught—hence his eponymous title.

The Earth mercenaries had managed to creep up on the powerful Martian warrior with a dart rifle while he had been sleeping it off in a back room of an off-world bar in a little-known corner of the Asteroid Belt. There were enough tranquilizers in the dart to put a grizzly bear to bed. All it had managed to do to the Martian was wake him up—the Earthlings had beaten a hasty retreat. In the end, they had managed to subdue him with three more darts fired by a sniper hired at the last minute using a long-distance sonar rifle equipped with night-vision telescopic sights. The Martian was still galloping towards them when the fourth dart went in. It did not look in a good mood as it (thankfully, for all concerned) finally collapsed.

They had sold him for a handsome profit to a slave trader who specialized in supplying gladiators to orbiting circuses— not, however, without considerable risk to themselves and the trader's foot soldiers. The Martian seemed intent on killing anybody or anything that made the mistake of getting within reach of his extremely long third arm. The trader's soldiers had finally managed to get an electric collar on him (Martians were particularly sensitive to electricity), and now they could disable him at the press of a button.

The Martian wasn't happy about it, but finally, and grudgingly, he learned that it was only used when he showed unwarranted aggression towards his captors. He could use as much aggression as he liked against his opponents in the gladiatorial ring, and that was something he did ruthlessly and systematically.

For a Martian warrior, the only honorable death lay in combat. It was number 42's only goal. The humans would not have understood. They thought he fought to stay alive, when, in fact, he fought only to die.

The fight had been slowly and deliberately built up. All of the Martian 42's gladiatorial battles had been off-world (meaning, far from the confines of the inner solar system and the so-called civilized orbiting planets). He was, therefore, a relatively unknown quantity. But as the encounter grew nearer, the hitherto trickle of information regarding 42 turned into a flood. It appeared that the Martian had participated in just as many fights as the Klatck and was therefore potentially as lethal. It had proved a cunning strategy by the promoters as it had now provoked solar-wide interest.

A biped, or even a powerful tri-ped (like a Martian), was no match for a Klatck at close quarters even armed with a high-powered laser canon. A Klatck resembled a huge bull or rhinoceros-like animal, though three times as big and exponentially as powerful. It had one horn, which was razor sharp; it could cut through steel like butter. The Klatck, like a bull, carried most of its bulk in its hind-quarters, and it was there that it generated maximum speed to use its terrible horn to horrendous effect. Its body was covered in thick, interlocking plates of hide as strong as iron, like a rhinoceros. Even its eyes were protected by a thick membrane. It was a bright, vivid red and was in a constant state of raging fury that only varied according to the object placed in front of it and how soon the Klatck could reduce said object to a mulch.

The combat would take place in an oval arena called the Solarineum, which was currently orbiting Earth. It was the largest orbiting gladiatorial circus in the system. Every few years, it would be positioned in orbit around one of the *civilized* planets by giant solar space tugs. The huge, squat, ugly ships, all engine and power, were readying themselves to haul the Solarineum to Venus once the combat was over and the spectators had departed. This was to be the main event and culmination of its one-hundredth anniversary as the greatest spectacle in the system. And to mark the special occasion, the two ambassadors from Venus and Earth were gracing the historic event.

At either end of the floor of the arena were two heavy metal doors through which the gladiators would make their entrance. The arena had sheer metal walls topped by a heavily proofed glass-fronted gallery that housed the audience. The audience, despite the outrageous cost, was already huge—somewhere in the many thousands; not to mention the media coverage that was beaming live to all of the populated planets. It was a historic event, not only because of the anniversary of the Solarineum and its extraordinary presentation, but also because it was the first time in many years that the two ambassadors from Earth and Venus had shared the same space.

The Martian named 42 was escorted to the holding cell behind the southernmost door of the arena by two heavily armed Venusians and two similarly armed Earthmen. Once inside the cell, he calmly limbered up by doing some stretches and checked over his laser cannon. It was fully powered and ready, although it would be about as effective as a pea shooter against a raging Klatck in full attack mode. He turned it around and tested its weight as a club—it wouldn't make much difference either way he used it.

The Martian sat down and patiently waited for the holding cell's door to the arena to open and the crowd's roar of anticipation of his certain death. He was perfectly calm, and if you could tell whether a Martian was smiling, then that was probably what 42 was doing. He was looking forward to his honorable death—the Klatck was a suitable adversary.

A red light above the door started to flash as it slowly drew upwards, revealing the empty arena. The crowd wanted to gape a while at the Martian before the Klatck was released. It wasn't often you got to see a Martian stormtrooper in the flesh unless you were an Imperial soldier or a mercenary, and then it was probably the last thing you ever saw.

The Martian strode slowly, upright and elegant, into the arena on its three hind limbs as if he were partaking of the air in a particularly picturesque flower garden. He carried the laser cannon cradled loosely in its center forward arm. This third and main limb split into three perfect and separate symmetrical arms, each with hands with nine long fingers, and it manipulated the canon and its instrument panel easily. The weight of the laser cannon would have made a human soldier bend double. It was normally used by the infantry as a mounted weapon and manned by at least two soldiers. The Martian named 42 carried it as if it were a twig.

The noise from the audience as 42 coolly made his appearance went up by several decibels, to which he seemed entirely indifferent. The Martian went to the center of the arena and waited patiently, rocking backwards and forwards on his hind limbs. He could have been gazing out to sea or looking over a beautiful vista for all the attention he was paying the audience, or the inevitable death he faced when the far door opened.

It wasn't what the Solarineum crowd was used to when a gladiatorial competition involving a Klatck, especially Big Larry, was concerned. Usually, the victim, euphemistically called the "opponent," ran around like a headless chicken, seeking any kind of egress, screaming their lungs out and vacating their loosened bowels to the jeers of the crowd.

The red light above the door at the far end of the tunnel was flashing. The door was slowly beginning to rise, and to spike up the anticipation, a shrill alarm began to wail. The discontented crowd began to cheer. Now they would see bloody mayhem, and the overly proud and haughty Martian warrior would at long last shed his dignity and be brought low. He would be reduced to a bloody, insignificant pulp as he rightly deserved for being so boring and displaying such a lack of temerity, and worst of all, for not providing the suitable amount of entertainment, i.e., bowel-emptying fear. There was no enjoyment in watching some species suffer untold agonies if they looked like they didn't even care—it took all the fun out of the thing.

The Klatck had been enraged even more than usual (if it were possible) by being heavily prodded with red-hot diamond-sharpened osmium lances. Big Larry burst out of the holding pen, snorting and grunting with pent-up fury. It stopped a moment while it adjusted its glaring, hate-filled crimson eyes to the light—better to see any potential object, alive or dead, on which it could vent its temper.

Some hundreds of meters away it spied the Martian who was nonchalantly regarding it as one might look upon a particularly harmless somnambulant bovine grazing in a meadow. The Martian named 42 was sitting back on its haunches and eying the Klatck speculatively. If he had been sitting in a nineteenth-century English country garden, he would no doubt have been sipping a cup of Earl Grey and smoking a pipe while contemplating the creation of a sonnet to pass the time. The thoughts of both of the aliens did not actually concern sonnets, delightful as they may be, as neither of them would have recognized one if it had been power-nailed to their foreheads. It was an example merely to demonstrate the emotion stirring in the breast of one of the noble combatants. The other's emotions could not readily be put into words, unless they were a hundred feet high and gleamed FURY in bright red. The Klatck roared and thundered around the arena a few times to see if there was anything more interesting than the Martian on display, but satisfied that it was just 42 that was going to bear the full brunt of its displeasure, it worked itself up into an even more suitable state of fury preparatory to rending and trampling and readied itself to charge. It was going to take a long run up to see how many times it could bounce the creature off the walls.

The Martian had not even moved its head. Number 42 seemed disinclined to move at all, in fact.

The Venusian ambassador was informing the Earth ambassador of the startling fact that the relaxed Martian was actually smiling. They were both concerned. They both had huge bets on the Klatck, and both had discovered to their mutual horror that they had both made them with what they had considered a very gullible bookmaker, and the Venusian had just found out on his vid-phone that their mutual bookmaker was merely a Martian stooge and was taking no more bets.

Number 42 stirred himself as if waking from a pleasant daydream and walked slowly towards the pawing Klatck before it began its much-anticipated charging. On the way, it tossed the laser cannon to one side. The Martian would face the Klatck empty-handed. Big Larry seemed surprised, if

Klatcks were capable of such an emotion. In fact, you could say it was positively taken aback. It was used to living things running away, not walking calmly towards it. Big Larry seemed confused for a second, and then it decided it was better to return to default mode and charged. The crowd cheered loudly, none more so than the ambassadors.

The Martian held his ground, empty-handed and still seemingly without a semblance of emotion. Then, just meters before Big Larry was sure to make its deadly, bone-crunching impact, the huge Klatck suddenly locked its front legs and unbelievably skidded to a halt just centimeters from the Martian's chest.

The crowd fell silent in disbelief. Nothing like this had ever happened before. Big Larry lowered its deadly horn and pointed it directly at number 42's neck. The crowd cheered once again. The Klatck was obviously just taking its time. It was going to prolong the agony of the Martian's death by goring him apart slowly. But instead, the Klatck very deliberately slipped the sharply pointed tip of its horn beneath the Martian's electric collar and deftly sliced it off. Then, with the Solarineum silent and completely stunned, Big Larry knelt as if in reverence to the Martian named number 42.

The Martian retrieved the laser cannon and mounted the Klatck's back. Then, before the guards had time to realize what was happening and close the door, Big Larry charged back to its holding cell. It charged straight through the cell door like a living tornado. There were a flash and explosion from laser cannon fire from inside the cell, and then the screaming began...Somehow the pair had managed to reach the gallery. There was pandemonium.

The ambassadors were quickly hustled away. Their mutual guards were shooting indiscriminately into the crowd in order to clear a path for the pair to the escape pods. They rapidly secured a two-man pod for the ambassadors by shooting the occupants and bundling the VIPs inside.

As the pod disengaged from the Solarineum, the ambassadors looked back at the view of the retreating orbiting circus. They could make out the chaos that was going on inside and the blood-red strips where the Klatck and its mounted Martian were wreaking carnage through the thousands of spectators. Judging by the mayhem, there were unlikely to be many survivors. The Solarineum would have to be gassed and quarantined.

The Earth ambassador turned to his Venusian counterpart. "Does this mean we lost the bet?"

THE SWEEPER AND THE SEA

Miguel navigated his way cautiously down the steep dunes onto the beach, avoiding as much as possible the many small, prickly thorn bushes that covered the white drifting sand. The salted sea wind stung his eyes and clouded his vision, as if he was walking through a cloud of toxic dust instead of windswept sand. The barren, uninterrupted shoreline stretched as far as one could see, or at least perceive, through the clouds of spray sent up by the roaring, breaking never-ceasing waves. The long rolls of the thunderous breakers provided a monotonous bass to the crash of the surf and the high-pitched eradicating hiss of the receding undertow, which could drag any living creature with it once it was within its grasp, down into its dark, glacial depths.

This stretch of the coast had always been ill-famed for its dangerously and fatally powerful undertow. The villagers knew it as a shiftless dark seam, a space between light and darkness. No one swam here who knew of this condition, not even the most adventurous surfers or divers, and no one came here except perhaps the odd passing tourist who had wandered from the established routes and was curious to see this wasted, barren landscape of the Caribbean shore where the land met the sea without mercy, or perhaps because it was a fitting finale to the fertile green rain forests and its resplendent outpouring of nature, this seemingly nonexistent plane where it was difficult to tell where earth met sea.

The only sign of life that existed on the windswept dunes were bedraggled clumps of sickly, stiff grass, and the thorn bushes, which all clung together as if in desperation against the fierce dehydrating blast from the ocean. The stricken plants were all a sickly grey-green. Many had died, their dried carcasses still clinging stubbornly to the sand, a testament to the obstinate force of survival; some seemed undecided, as if they hadn't arrived at a permanent decision whether they should put forth the strenuous effort of growing more leaves or simply stifle and wither along with their stricken comrades and remain as mummified corpses of what had once been life.

The small village, which Miguel came from, a mile or so from this forsaken beach, and where the sea was strangely settled and calm, was nestled in a small bay. It consisted mainly of small adobe and stone houses painted (for those that could afford paint) in a bizarre variety of colors according to the owner's preference and loosely spread around the base of a low and flat, featureless mountain.

It was a fishing village, always had been, clinging to the base of the mountain like a stubborn barnacle; no one was rich there, or even moderately wealthy, but the villagers didn't mind; they led a quiet, settled life, punctuated only by the days of bad weather when the sea raged even in their quiet harbor. Sometimes it stretched its unforgiving limbs to nearly reach their small havens, and then it was impossible to fish or even venture outside. The boats would be hauled up alongside their dwellings, and every fisherman, in turn, helped their neighbors to tow their small, simple, but streamlined vessels to the safety of their respective dwellings. On those days, the village men would play dominoes in darkened rooms and drink white rum while the women chatted amongst themselves or busied themselves with household chores.

There were a small church and an equally small graveyard near the top of the barren mountain, filled with the empty graves of fishermen who had never returned home. Some, who had survived the sea to die of old age, were buried alongside their wives, with the earth alongside already reserved for their descendants, but there still remained many widows, ritually mourning their departed husbands' absences every Sunday, dressed in the eponymous, dark black uniforms of widows.

It was somewhat distant from the usually quiet waters of the village, on the desolate shore on the other side of the mountain, where Miguel now stumbled towards the raging seas. It was a place populated only by the lost souls of the drowned, who had either mistaken the sea as being suitable for swimming or fisherman who had strayed into the unforgiving currents. It was there that a solitary young woman named Maria scraped out a living.

Miguel had known Maria since they were children. They had gone to school together, if you could call the open hut with its one solitary classroom in the middle of the village a school. It was where children of all ages and even the occasional adults were taught the basics of the alphabet and sums. She was an orphan of one of the many dead fishermen and his wife, a wife who had calmly walked into the sea to be taken within its cold embrace on hearing of the death of her husband. She had been brought up by her aunt in a small, rickety, makeshift shack at the end of the unfrequented beach, where she lived still, now alone, her aunt long-since dead.

At school, there had been no obvious signs of the madness that was to follow as she grew older. Some said it was because of living alone on the haunted, isolated beach, away from the village's calmer waters and human presence. The more elderly in the village maintained that it had always run in the family.

Maria, the last in the line of her misfit family, had left school early and had spent her time beachcombing, scavenging washed-up wood and supplies for her aunt, who, between them, somehow managed to eke out a living from the windswept wasteland; they lived mostly off seaweed and washed-up fish. They would collect driftwood, from which her aunt would fashion simple household objects, sculptures, and strange objects that would spring from her unique imagination, some of which they would occasionally manage to sell for a pittance at the weekly village market.

Even at the village school, Maria had been morose, speaking little and given to sudden outbursts of violent temper. Gradually she had withdrawn into herself, silent and non-committal, and now no one in the village could remember if she had ever spoken at all.

It was shortly after her aunt died, when Maria was still barely a teenager, that she had developed the eccentric behavior that earned her the local title of *La Loca*. She had taken to the futilitarian task of sweeping back the ocean's waves with a worn-out broom; a sort of modern-day female Canute.

At first, the villagers found this behavior amusing, believing it to be a harmless passing fad that children might pass through, like roller skating or kite flying, but as she got older, it had stopped being considered merely eccentric and was now considered just plain madness.

Her mental disorder, such as it was, did not stop the fishermen from the village paying her perfidious nocturnal visits. The few coins they left her meant that she could occasionally make a small purchase in the village, where she was shunned by the local women and tormented by the children, who would throw pebbles at her bare feet and call her names, most of which they did not know the meaning of but which they had overheard their parents using in whispered, spiteful voices whenever *La Loca* was mentioned.

When he had heard the men describing their use of her in the local bar, Miguel had felt his face reddening, and he'd had to turn away. He did not know whether it was from shame, jealousy, or anger. He was one of the only young men who had never taken advantage of her availability.

There, shimmering in the distance, Miguel could just make out the ragged, scarecrow figure running along the surf's edge. She was barefoot and dressed in her usual tattered, dark rags, which resembled the seaweed of the shore, and parts of it probably were. He shouted out her name, but it was whipped away by the wind as if he had merely whispered it. He cursed, bent his head once again against the fierce blast, and pushed his way through the eternal sandstorm, down the dunes to the beach.

As usual on his many visits, he had brought her a gift: a slab of the village's dark, rich homemade chocolate, wrapped in newspaper. He had once made the mistake of bringing her a new broom, a bright red plastic model he had bought in the market. He had found it destroyed the next day on the rock where he had left it.

Normally, he would leave the chocolate on the rock and return to the village. It was impossible to get any kind of reaction from Maria when she was sweeping. Miguel did not mind. He respected her privacy. He knew he could never be like the other men from the village who gave her those few pesos in return for a night in her shack. In some ways, he was proud of that, but it did not stop his longing for her, and even though a young man, he was still a virgin; his imagination of the act made his longing even more painful to bear. He cared about her, and her bizarre behavior did nothing to change that. But today was different. Today he needed to speak with her. He had something important to tell her.

Tomorrow he was leaving for the city. His uncle had found him a job in a tire factory. He would make the long journey by the monthly train that wound its way serpent-like through the thick green overgrowth of the jungle. He would not miss the village, but he would miss her. He would miss the silent recognition in her dark, deep eyes. The recognition that only the solitary and lonely felt.

He hurried along the surf line. Even though she was near him now, the spray from the crashing waves enveloped her in a jeweled mist so that she appeared as nothing more than a vague, quickly moving shadow, like a fish moving through water.

She was marching swiftly up and down the shore. Every so often, she used the old broom to push back the relentless waves into the sea. Her face was expressionless, as always, while she performed the futile task. Her wild, long black hair danced around her head, blown in all directions by the wind as if it had a life of its own, and her cheeks ran wet with the salt spray.

He caught up with her and grabbed her arm. She offered no resistance, merely stared up at his face from beneath her long tresses as he babbled out his story. His eyes searched hers for some sort of reaction, a reaction of any kind that meant she might miss him. Wordlessly, she took his hand and led him up the path to her lonesome dwelling, built from the detritus of the sea itself.

It was still dark when he left, the Bible-black darkness of the dead of night. He had wanted to leave her some money, but she had replaced it in his pocket and kissed him lightly on his cheek.

As he walked out of the darkness of the shack, he felt no shame. He would return for her—he had promised her that. He registered only slight surprise as his feet became wet from the rising water. Underneath the black, calm surface of the sea, he could make out the still-dancing amber lamps of his distant village as though it was at the bottom of an aquarium filled with diffuse light. Each house glowed with its own sub-aquatic light as if in celebration of finally being beneath the sea where it had always belonged. The oil lamps glimmered like stars reflected in an ebony pool. He felt he could reach out to touch them as he was silently swallowed, embraced by the rising, dark depths of the sea.

Many years later, a sailor sweeping the decks of a foreign cargo ship that had drifted off course and found itself on that desolate shore swore that he saw mellow lights in the depths and the outlines of small, quaintly painted cottages. He told those who would listen that it seemed to him that he had seen people moving down below, going about their everyday business, and, on a hill, a beautiful woman with long, flowing hair embraced a young man and waved happily at him. It seemed to the sailor that her arm grew longer and longer as if it were reaching out to him and was preparing to drag him down into the depths. He threw his broom at her and ran along the deck. Only once did he look back, and it was to see the woman clutching the broom in triumph as the seas grew murky once again and the vision disappeared.

THE TATTOOIST

Sir Charles Manning was one of the twentieth century's most celebrated artists. He was also one of the century's greatest forgers, but this was conveniently forgotten when he was knighted by Her Majesty. Amongst his many talents was also that of plastic surgery. He had begun his career in the medical profession, but after becoming famous as an artist, he performed only private and aesthetic operations. He amassed a vast fortune during his lifetime but never got married or had children; hence, there were no heirs to his fortune when he died.

Manning possessed, amongst other idiosyncratic qualities, a very twisted sense of humor and a genuine love of puzzles and cryptography. His twisted sense of humor came to the fore when his will was read. He left his works of art, the legal ones (he was a skilled counterfeiter), and his huge mansion to the state to be preserved in his memory. He also left millions in bonds, diamonds, and cash to whoever could figure out by means of his works of art where they were located, and then they, the finder, would be the legal owner of all the aforementioned treasure.

The National Trust, to whom the mansion and works of art had been entrusted, was entirely unprepared for the reaction from the more nefarious members of the public. The mansion was ransacked so many times by criminal treasure seekers that the cost of the extra security and maintenance far outweighed the money coming in from honest visitors. The

Trust sold the works of art to various public galleries and put the mansion up for sale; however, they did not receive any offers, no one wanted a place so subject to burglaries, and the place fell into ruin.

One of the many people who were interested in the treasure was a certain Mr. Lancelot Grey. He was not a common member of the underground but a self-made millionaire who also happened to be as interested in puzzles and cryptography as Sir Charles had been. He liked the idea of becoming richer, although he really did not need the money or the work involved to get it, but the challenge set by the eccentric artist was too interesting for him to resist.

He had paid several visits to the mansion when it had been open to the public and studied Manning's artwork very closely. He had even managed to see every one of the paintings in private collections as well, by either paying their proprietors or ingratiating himself with them. He had photographs, prints, and books on every piece of artwork Manning had ever done. He also knew about the forgeries and had studied those; he had even bought a couple for himself. After three years of careful study, he found himself no nearer to finding the secret that would lead him to the treasure, and he had become slowly but surely obsessed with the quest.

Grey realized that this was turning into a kind of *Da Vinci Code* thing, but there seemed to be nothing he could do about it. His wife had left him to live with her mother and said she wouldn't come back until he had regained his senses. His fortune was finally starting to dwindle, and finding the treasure had now become a financial necessity as well as a personal quest. After fruitlessly studying every piece of art that Manning had ever done, from rough sketches and dawdles to full-scale works of art, he decided to go back to the beginning. Somewhere along the line, he decided, he had missed something of vital importance.

Manning had started painting relatively late in his career and, as previously mentioned, was a successful surgeon before specializing in plastic surgery; perhaps it was his expert knowledge of anatomy that made his human figures so lifelike and convincing. In that way, Manning was very similar to Da Vinci. And then Grey stumbled onto something extraordinary. It seemed that Manning, whilst studying medicine, had worked as a tattooist's assistant to earn his keep.

The tattoo shop was still in business, although it was now run by the son. The son was susceptible to financial gain, and after Grey had parted with several twenty-pound notes, he promised to look through his father's designs to see if there were any attributable to Manning. Grey also promised to help the son in the verification and sale of said designs if they should be discovered.

The son actually managed to unearth Manning's employment record when he had worked at the shop. It seemed his father had been a meticulous bookkeeper. Amongst his father's tattoo designs, the son discovered some that had been drawn by Manning. Grey studied them all closely, including those of the tattooist, but he still came no closer to the discovery he was hoping for. After having them evaluated, he agreed to buy them off the son. There was one that was of particular interest to him as it gave a clear indication of the artist's style that was to follow.

All of Manning's work contained intricate hidden messages, which it took some time to work out, hence the years of study that were usually devoted to him and were now being devoted to seeking out his treasure.

The tattoo design that particularly interested Grey was of a very sexual nature. It depicted a kind of transsexual in the throes of ecstasy. Something in the design sparked a memory of his studies of Manning's life, but he couldn't quite put his finger on it.

One night, it came to him: in later years, Manning's now mainly aesthetic interest in plastic surgery had been of a purely sexual nature. He had solely performed sex reassignment, male to female, operations. He had his own private clinic where he performed some of the aforesaid operations himself. It had an excellent reputation and was not unduly expensive.

The male and female figures were always prominent in his paintings, and many were transgender. Then the most extraordinary idea came to Grey. What if it were all somehow linked? Had Manning hidden a tattoo, pointing the way to his treasure, in one of his manufactured vaginas? It was not beyond the twisted imagination of Manning; in fact, it would positively appeal to him. This strange and perhaps perverted idea took a strong hold on Grey because of the simple reason it was SO Manning.

Grey was faced with a problem, as the clinic was still practicing, and access to the patient's records would thus be illegal and prohibited. He was now quite low on funds as he had neglected his business to the point of bankruptcy in search of his Holy Grail, and bribing a member of the staff would be out of the question. He had also succumbed to the demon drink, and when not in avid pursuit of some clue, he doused his sorrows and frustration with alcohol.

In this case, however, his inebriation came to the rescue. He had become determined to break into the clinic and find the records of Manning's operations, but he could leave no trace of the break-in or that the records had been removed as it would put his competitors on the same trail. Up to then, Grey had not resorted to out-and-out criminal acts, but he was desperate. He had no knowledge of how to perform a burglary, but he knew there was such a thing as "staking out the joint."

So, night after night and day after day, he would spend long hours surveying the clinic until he was familiar with its routines and its members of staff. So it was that one night, whilst quenching his thirst in a pub near the clinic, he recognized the clinic's night watchman. He befriended him over the following weeks by buying him drinks, which the watchman was quite happy to accept. It wasn't long before Grey was visiting him at his job at the clinic in the early hours with a flask of something to "warm the cockles." He had convinced the watchman that he, Grey, was an insomniac and he'd rather pass the night in pleasant conversation than tossing and turning in his bed.

It was through these nocturnal visits that Grey became familiar with the layout of the clinic and knew where the records of past operations were kept. On an appropriate evening when the watchman usually imbibed more than others (it being the end of his week's shift), he slipped the night watchman a "Mickey Finn," as Grey had heard them termed.

As soon as the night watchman drifted off to sleep, Grey slipped swiftly into the registry office and found all the files he wanted and photocopied them. He returned them all exactly as he had found them and then left the clinic, never to return.

He spent months of painstaking research with the files, which practically drove the last strands of sanity from his overtaxed brain. It didn't help that he was now completely reliant on alcohol and drugs just to make it through the day. He lived in a squalid bedsit with barely enough money to eat. But finally, the files gave up the information he had so desperately been seeking and a way out of his desperate situation.

Grey had placed all the sex reassignment operations that Manning himself had performed in chronological order. They were all basically the same, details of who had performed the surgery, the length of the operation, and the name of the patient and their details followed by the date they had left the clinic.

One morning, bleary-eyed and unshaven, he started his usual routine of drinking and searching through the files. He was nearly at the end of them now and was dreading the day when he would finally find this was yet another dead end.

He carefully read the details of the surgery. The patient was a twenty-four-year old transsexual named Peter Gillies. He had undergone a full vaginoplasty, which gave him/her a fully sensitive vagina.

Manning first removed the testicles, and then he'd slit the penis long ways and inverted it. Then, along with a small piece of the foreskin, he'd provided a hood for the glans of the penis, which were converted into the vagina's clitoris. This clitoris was fully supplied with nerve endings and, therefore, completely innervated and would provide adequate sexual stimulus. Manning then used the rest of the foreskin, along with scrotal tissue from which he had removed the pubic hair follicles, to create the labia minora.

It was here that Grey's heart skipped a beat. Manning had written a personal note at the bottom of the formal document in the comments' section describing how he had inked a small tattoo on the labia minora at the patient's request. He'd also added that it was a unique tattoo, the design of which the patient had left wholly in his hands. Even the nurses and the anesthetist had not been privy to the final work.

This was it! Grey trembled, and not just with the DTs, as he held the precious document in his hand. He had found the hidden clue that would lead him finally to the answer he had so stubbornly sought, and subsequently his fortune. And then the reality hit him: how the hell was he going to find Peter Gillies, or for that matter, whatever she called herself after the operation?

In fact, it turned out easier than he thought. The patient, formerly known as Peter Gillies, had signed her release form with what was obviously a poorly practiced and new signature. As such, it was simple enough to decipher as Julie Gillies. The internet can be a wonderful tool in the right hands, and Grey had become something of an expert over the years in tracking down obscure information and references. He had Gillies's name, date of birth, and place of birth—that was a wealth of information in internet terms; with a little bit of money and some know-how, he tracked down Julie Gillies pretty easily. She was working as a drag artist in a seedy club in Soho.

Lancelot Grey lost no time in becoming a member of the less-than-salubrious club. He planned on courting Julie Gillies (in the most gentlemanly way), but in the end, all it took was buying her a few cocktails after her act. Before he knew it, he was back at her place, and she was all over him. He had prepared himself with plenty of Viagra for just such an eventuality, not because he found Julie Gillies particularly unattractive, but because alcohol was now causing him serious erectile problems. Ms Gillies was enchanted by Grey's apparent enthusiasm and even more enchanted when he expressed the desire to perform cunnilingus on her. And she could not have been more pleased when he told her to leave the light on. In her experience, most men couldn't wait to put the light out fast enough.

She started to get a bit suspicious when the man who had called himself Gary (obviously a false name as he did not look like a Gary—far too posh) seemed to be spending an inordinate amount of time peering into her vagina instead of licking it like he had promised.

"Hey, what you doing down there?" she blurted out. "Drawing a picture? Less looking, more licking, please."

"Oh, it's just that I thought I saw something, like a beautiful picture."

"That's strange because I've got a tattoo down there, but you can't see it. I've tried lots of times with a mirror. It's too far inside me. It was done by that famous artist guy Manning. He always told me that every time I made love with a man in the future, I should tell them that they had been inside a true work of art."

She suggestively rubbed her muscular and slightly hairy leg against Grey. Unfortunately, the Viagra wasn't working as advertised. Grey suppressed a shudder.

"Are you an art lover, darling?" Julie asked, trying to suppress a yawn.

"Yes," Grey said. "I am, much more than you could possibly know."

With no little relief, he disengaged himself from between the transsexual's legs. The Mickey Finn appeared to be finally having the desired effect on Ms. Gillies. She had fallen into a deep, snoring sleep. Grey then injected her with a syringe full of morphine to knock her out completely. It would be painless for her. She would never have to wake up to see the horror that had been left between her legs.

He went to work with a cut-throat razor and scalpel. It was hard going, but he got his prize out perfectly intact. He thought Manning himself might have been impressed with his work. He left with the only remaining unknown piece of art by Sir Charles Manning, wrapped in newspaper, in a plastic carrier bag half-filled with ice.

THE PRISONER

She never knew, nor understood, why they suddenly took her. There were thousands of homeless in the city they could have picked. She was also very young at the time. All she could remember were some men in dark coats jumping out of a van and bundling her into its rear. They put something over her head, something that blotted out all light, sound, and smell except its own smell, which was of strong disinfectant and nothing much else. No one helped or even took much notice. Things like that were common-place in the city. People were afraid to intervene. You could smell the fear.

Her mother, from what she could remember of her, had always warned of her the possibility that she might be taken. She had taught her to blend into the background as much as possible, to seek refuge where people seldom ventured, to seek invisibility. But her mother had one day disappeared, and thereafter she had had to learn the lessons of survival on the street by herself. She did not know her own name, did not even know if she had ever been given one.

She had been raped more times than she could remember, sometimes by gangs, all fighting to take their turn on her, but luckily, she had never fallen pregnant. She knew how to avoid those traps pretty well. The gangs had their own territories. Lone ravagers were more difficult; they came out of nowhere, like the van.

Things might have been different if one of them had been kind and befriended her, but they never did. She was just a body to be used. A hole to momentarily satiate their lust.

That was all she could remember now. If it could be called a memory. Sometimes she was not sure that it had really happened at all. Perhaps it had all been a dream, although she seldom dreamt, and if she did, she never remembered them—perhaps that was a blessing.

She had pleaded with her unknown captors to be returned to the streets, but she was ignored. She was chained to a wall permanently to prevent her escape. She supposed she was in some kind of prison, although there appeared to be no other inmates. If there were, she could not hear them and she had good hearing.

The men who arrived to give her food and water in the small cell where they kept her were impervious to her supplications. They did not even seem to understand her language. They did know how to kick, though.

The food they gave her, if it could be called that, was thrown to her in bowls on the floor and consisted of an awful mashed paste that smelled and tasted like nothing she had ever tried. She had found better food at the bottom of garbage cans, but eventually she had to eat as her stomach groaned for sustenance.

As she grew older and stronger, she tried to attack one of her guards. She was severely beaten, and her food ration more than halved; by the time she was on the verge of starvation, she was fed again.

She realized she had become absolutely submissive now; all her street smarts had deserted her. Now she was just a beggar; a beggar who would do anything just to remain alive. In some way, this made her feel better inside. Survival was something she understood. She even crawled over to one of the men and licked his boots. The man only laughed and kicked her in the stomach. She cried, begged her forgiveness; she didn't understand what it was that she had done wrong, but she begged all the same.

She settled into the routine of the prison. Her food times were the only thing she looked forward to even though the stuff they gave her was awful and only seemed to vary in how disgusting it was, but still her stomach would unaccountably yearn for it.

She had thought it could not get worse for her than her life was at that moment. But it did, for instead of the guards in black overalls, there now appeared men in white coats who had her restrained while they stuck very pointy sharp things in her that stung and made her cry out in pain. Afterwards she had terrible visions and could not sleep for days, and her shit ran down her legs like piss.

They came up with seemingly new tortures every day. The spiky things did different things to her, which the men muttered about amongst themselves in their strange language. Some days, she spent the whole time vomiting. On others, she was blasted with noise until she thought her eardrums would burst. Nearly every fortnight, she was spun in a strange machine that so totally disoriented her she could barely stand for days. Just like the men in black, they ignored her pleas every time they arrived. She tried to speak to them. It was clear they did not want to understand. They talked amongst themselves in hushed whispers, eyeing her all the while in a cold, special language that was theirs only and lacked any emotion.

Her excrement and vomit lined the walls and floor of the cramped empty cell. It was devoid of any furniture. There was no bed, not even a blanket. Every few days, the men in black hosed down the cell with powerful jets of cold water. She would cower and whimper in a corner and try to cover her naked body as the freezing jet of water pinned her to the wall. Then she was left shivering on the floor until she was eventually dry and warmth returned to her body.

She had ceased to cry a long time ago. It seemed that she had lost the capacity to feel sorry for herself, or even to plead with her captors for mercy. They had never shown the slightest sign of empathy at any time, and it did not look like that was about to change.

A day arrived when she could sense a change in the atmosphere. The guards in their black apparel were tenser and more on edge than usual, and even the men in white coats for once seemed to be behaving with some small show of kindness to her. They whispered words in her ears in their strange language that seemed to hold feelings of encouragement hinged with trepidation. Were they about to kill her? If so, she was too tired to put up even the slightest degree of resistance. She would just close her eyes and go to sleep...

The reason for this unusual behavior became quickly apparent: men dressed very differently had arrived, and she somehow sensed these clothes inspired fear and trepidation in the other men. They were all heavily perfumed, she noticed, nicer smells than the strong soaps, disinfectant, and bleach she was used to. All the guards, she observed, just through their body language, treated them with mute respect and stood very straight.

These new arrivals, who all had hair on their lips, eyed her up and down. They touched her naked body and felt her parts; she knew better now than to react, but at least their touches were tender for a change. One even went so far as to stroke her cheek, run his fingers through her hair, and murmur something that sounded gentle and sweet. She had to restrain herself from kissing the hand of this man who stroked her flesh with such delicacy that it made her shudder with pleasure. It stirred long-ago memories of love that she had given but never received in turn.

They spoke to each other in their strange language that she still not could understand, but she sensed when they spoke to the others that their words held great weight. They always nodded obediently at these men, as if to argue with them would be impossible. Then they were gone as suddenly as they had arrived, to the obvious relief of the remaining personnel.

The next day, everything changed. She was taken to a different holding cell, not much better than the previous one but much more sanitized. The overpowering smell of disinfectant made her choke. Now all the men who came into the cell were dressed head to foot in strange white costumes that ballooned around their bodies. Their faces were covered in rubber masks that made them wheeze when they moved or breathed. She cowered in the corner as they wheeled in strange-looking machines that had flashing lights and leads that they attached to various parts of her body. She moaned as they clipped them on, but the wheezing men went on with their preparations methodically, ignoring whatever pain their work inflicted. What fresh torture were they preparing for her? She shut her mind down and lay submissively as they went about their business on her body. She had learned there was no point in resistance. Astonishingly enough, after a while, she felt nothing, but the men seemed very intent on their machines. Sometimes it was as if she had been forgotten altogether or become invisible. Perhaps something had gone wrong with them. Maybe the unnatural balloon men were ill. She hoped so. The days continued like this, if they were days or nights; she had long ago lost all sense of time. The burning bright lights had never been turned off since she had arrived at this terrible place. It was always midday.

One day, or night, the balloon men arrived with even more apparatus. They wheezed for several hours as they fitted the mysterious sticks together. Then, with a flick of a switch, the metal machines glowed and sparkled.

She was forced to wear something heavy over her head now for hours on end. It made her neck ache. She could only hear the sound of her own breathing, and the air tasted funny as if it, too, was made of rubber like the balloon men. Perhaps there was something wrong with *her* and not *them*, a disease, maybe, it would explain a lot of things. Then the balloon-men brought in a leather-clad metal chair. It must have been very heavy because they wheezed a lot.

It had been a long time since she had seen a chair. She had almost forgotten what they looked like. But this was a very strange chair; it did not look like any chair she had ever seen, and it smelled strongly of the balloon men.

They put some sort of leather harness around her and strapped her into the large, metallic chair. As usual, she put up no resistance. She sensed death around her and started to cry. It had been so long since she had cried that she hadn't realized that she was still capable of it. She wailed out the simplest question: "Why?" She cried it over and over again. But nothing seemed to deter the wheezing men. They never even paused in whatever task they were performing.

More injections followed. She had had so many now that they had difficulty finding her veins. It hurt, and she cried a little, although she knew it would do no good. They did eventually manage to get a needle in, and catheters and tubes were connected. Then, worst of all, the balloon men placed the heavy thing over her head and clicked switches. Then all was darkness.

She had not been in such darkness for so long that it terrified her more than anything else she had been through. It was darker than the darkest night. She struggled to break free, but it was all in vain; she was so securely strapped she couldn't move a muscle, not even her neck. She could not cry out as the helmet thing muzzled her mouth. She could only breathe through her nose, and now she found herself wheezing like the balloon men.

The thing they had put over her head started to smell strange as if it was contaminated inside. The air smelled different, more like chemicals than the rubbery smell of the balloon men. She had to exert herself to breathe. It made her ribs ache like they were being slowly crushed from the outside. She felt like one of the wheezing balloon men. The hollow sound of her desperate breathing echoed around her skull in time with the thumping pain of her heart that felt like it wanted to burst out of her chest.

All the pain stopped, and she felt like she was floating through the air. She basked in the absence of feeling. In her head, she called this sensation: *NO PAIN*. It was the best feeling in the world.

They were moving her somewhere. She could sense it even though her body lacked any sensation now. It seemed to take a very long time; their movement was not much faster than the slowest walking pace. She had not been used to moving for so long, apart from her short exercise walks (when her legs were strong enough to bear her weight) around the confines of her tiny cell, but she knew by instinct she was going somewhere else. Somewhere outside the prison. And wherever it was, it was being done very slowly and with exaggerated care.

She then found himself rising and rising. She knew it because it was if her very guts were being left behind her. She had felt it once before but could not remember when. It was so unnerving she had difficulty breathing and had to learn to time her breaths; otherwise, it seemed like she would vomit out her heart. She wanted to vomit, but the thing they had placed over her head prevented her from even doing that. She had to swallow it back down; otherwise, she would choke, which made the waves of nausea when they came even worse. She felt she was being placed in some kind of container. She could now hear muffled voices in the background, but she was not sure if they came from inside her own head or from outside.

So, this was the end, then. She had no experience of death. She was the same as any being on the planet in that way, but she could sense its presence all around her.

A roaring noise filled her ears which even the contraption on her head could not contain. The world shook. She could feel her body slipping away from her. All was darkness, and then she lost consciousness. She was surprised when she regained it. But all was the same except that the tubes that had been inserted into her body pulsed. It seemed like the tubes were pumping things into her body. She felt the horrible taste of the paste as it was squirted down her throat. She swallowed it straight down as it was better not to dwell too much on the taste.

Time carried on in this manner. It was as if she were floating in a dark void that was only interrupted when the tubes pumped the obnoxious sustenance into her body. Other tubes pumped stuff to wake her up, others to send her to sleep, and others took all her waste products away.

She felt herself getting hot, and the heat seemed to be coming from inside her. It was becoming more and more difficult to breathe, and the more she tried, the more difficult it became. She could feel her heart pounding as she started to gasp. Then it was darkness, but this time, it was permanent.

Laika, the first dog in outer space, would no doubt have been enormously surprised (if she could have recognized herself, which dogs cannot) to have seen the small monument in her honor that was built near the military research facility in Moscow that prepared Laika's flight into space. It features a dog standing on top of a rocket.

Laika, no doubt, would have much preferred a loving pat on the head and a decent bowl of food. But who asks a dog?

COMETH THE FLOOD

I had this recurring dream when I was a kid. I must have been about nine or ten when I started having it. It was only when I was older that I realized why I had the dream.

I would wake up sometime after midnight with a slight pain in my bladder and a need to urinate. I would put on my dressing gown and slippers and go to use our outside toilet (it was a very old house). Bleary-eyed and still half asleep, I would return to my small, warm bed. I was practically asleep as soon as my head touched the pillow.

The special dream would usually come later on in the early hours of the morning, just when I was entering deep REM sleep. I had a kind of ritual I would use to enter this deep sleep world. I was only half conscious that I was doing it, but it always had a reassuring feel as if I were being cradled by a strong adult who could protect me from anything and anyone. It was a good feeling even though I knew the outcome was always the same and always bad.

I would keep my eyes tightly shut and imagine a tiny old man going around inside a roomy house that was my head, closing cupboards and shutting creaking doors that pertained to the organs and limbs of my body. I could feel them physically relax as the old man locked their control rooms up for the night.

I could hear his footsteps clearly as he thumped up and down the wooden stairs that connected the different landings of my mind—he wore large, heavy farming boots that announced each of his heavy steps.

I could join the old man at any time during his nightly rounds, entering the different rooms that operated my brain and body through the narrowest of doors and along the twisting, convoluted corridors of my mind, which were then firmly shut behind me. These rooms held the mystical machinery that controlled the different parts of my body. Switches would be turned off one by one, and levers pulled or released until I could no longer keep up and I heard the old man's footsteps receding into the distance of my mind, getting softer with each step. That was how I would fall into a deep sleep.

Then came the second part of my dream: once the house and all its rooms had been securely locked, I stepped outside.

It was always raining outside the house, a gentle never-ending rain. There was no sight of land in any direction, just the tops of trees. I would climb into my boat, except it was not a boat—it was a wardrobe. I had no need for oars. The wardrobe travelled quickly on the flood tides down tree-lined canals and across vast water-filled fields. There were no people, no animals, and no birds, just the blue-grey sky and water and the tops of trees swaying in time to my breathing. I sat upright in my wardrobe with the door open. It was quite comfortable. The vast expanses of water hardly ever changed until I was nearing the end of my dream.

The water would speed up as if we were reaching a waterfall or some rapids. The wardrobe would begin to rock from side to side. I traversed canals and rivers at ever increasing speeds. It was difficult to see the horizon anymore.

The sky and the water had become one. And that's when I would wake up with an even more urgent need to pee than earlier. I knew I would never make it to the outside toilet. But rather than wet the bed, I had found a temporary solution. I would pee in the narrow gap between my wardrobe and the wall. I would then climb back into my warm bed with a guilty conscience. Later, during the day, I would wipe the wall with a damp cloth and some disinfectant. Luckily, the old farmhouse where we lived was susceptible to damp, and no one took much notice of the stains on my wall. The slight smell of urine was put down to my granddad, who slept in the room next door and used a bed pan for his business.

The wet part of my dream stopped when we moved house and we had a toilet on the same landing. The old man still performed his nightly vigil, but gradually and imperceptibly he, too, disappeared.

In my late teens, I found a new way of falling into the welcome embrace of sleep. I had a small yellow transistor radio, which, when I was tripping on acid, I would find had a kind smiling face, and out of its mouth issued forth the most delightful music. I lived on the coast then, and I could pick up the pirate-radio ship *Mi Amigo's* broadcast: Radio Caroline. It broadcast, according to the blurb "*The latest in experimental and psychedelic music,*" which, in those days, meant people like Pink Floyd, Tangerine Dream, Jethro Tull when they were just starting out, that sort of thing. I used to feel in the darkness of the small hours that I was the only one listening to that strange, secret music. It made me feel good inside, and I would fall asleep with the radio quietly humming its sweet rock to me through the night. The bands became popular, and I got old.

I am in my fiftieth year now, and the floods of my boyhood dreams have turned into reality. I have had to move all my stuff upstairs as the bottom half of my house is under nearly a foot of stagnant water. I sometimes wish I was still with my sweet Filipino girlfriend, Marisol. Mind you, she would not have enjoyed all the rain, but she would have helped me so much with the domestic chores. She was a fiercely hardworking woman. No, in these sorts of circumstances, my ex-wife, Sharon, would have been much more useful. She was half German and had a stoic attitude to whatever life threw at her. Unfortunately, she also had itchy feet, and our marriage only lasted for three years. She was not really the kind of woman to settle down, and at the end of the day, I was pretty much a homebody. I did like my women, though, and I never had any difficulty finding willing females to share my bed.

You must think I am a kind of Lothario. I suppose I am in a way. As I said, I've never had any problem getting my end away. I am tall, and my body has been made strong, tanned, and weathered by the healthy work of the fields. I've got a full head of blonde hair bleached nearly white by the sun, and I know my blue eyes crinkle in a seducing smile when I want them to. But I'm particular about my women. I've never gone much for any of the village lasses (most were obese and serial scrubbers); that was far too easy and, at the same time, far too complicated. There is too much gossip in villages, and you end up getting caught up in it—snared like a rabbit. No, I preferred foreign women, the more exotic the better. I also liked my women to be independent, no ties.

They came to live in my small cottage, staying as long as they or I needed them to without bothering with the village too much.

The rain had started a couple of weeks ago, and there hadn't really been a let-up in the wet weather. Now we considered ourselves lucky in the village when it was just merely drizzling. The days and nights when it rained seemed as if the world had been turned upside down and the oceans, lakes, and rivers were emptying themselves solely upon our tiny plot of England. Luckily for me, I didn't live right down in the village centre, where they had been hardest hit. A lot of people had been evacuated. I lived some way out, peripheral to the village, on top of a small rise, but I still hadn't escaped the floods completely.

From my bedroom window, I could see Westbury Farm, where I had worked a good part of my life. Most of the land was under several feet of water, and I was worried. I had tried phoning the Cheswicks, who owned the farm, but the lines were down. They lived alone in the large, ramshackle farmhouse, as they had since as far back as most people in the village could remember. They were as much a part of the village as the land they had tilled faithfully all their lives. I could see the flood-water was pretty deep around the house because the surrounding land was flat and dipped slightly towards the other bloated river. The village had the misfortune of being in a valley between two rivers; it was a beautiful place, and it had been hundreds of years since it had flooded, but then it had been hundreds of years since it had rained like this.

I knew what I had to do; I had to check they were all okay in the farmhouse. The trouble was, I didn't have any kind of watercraft or even waders, and my wellington boots were too short and would just fill with water. I wasn't a strong swimmer either, and water frightened me, but I had to do something.

I went down the damp stairs to my open-plan living-come-dining room and surveyed the disaster that had once been the ground floor. The pattern of the carpet was just visible under the dirty water, which seemed to contain all kinds of flotsam and debris from God knows where.

Then I was struck by a bizarre idea. My dining room table was a large Ikea-type pine job; it was a light table—that meant it could float. I remember when Michelle, a beautiful French hitchhiker I had picked up one day, had given it to me. Even though it was a large table, she had managed to carry the whole flat-pack in by herself; so if I turned it upside down, I could sit on it and part paddle, part float down to the farm-house. Stranger things had been done in times of crisis. And I really needed to get down there. I also wanted to see from the upper floor of the farmhouse the state of the fields I loved.

I would have a far better view from up there as a line of hedges and trees at the bottom of my lane obscured the full view of the farmland from my cottage.

No sooner thought than done. I put my idea into action. It was surprisingly easy. Once I was a hundred-odd feet from my house, the water was deep enough for the table to float and also comfortably support my weight. I used a dustpan as a makeshift paddle. I would have presented an incongruous figure if there had been anyone around to see me, but the only sign of life was some crows squawking rancorously from the uppermost branches of the submerged trees; I imagine it was in rage at not being able to raid the precious land for seeds, or maybe they were just laughing.

It took me nearly half an hour to reach the house, and part of the time, I had to fight what appeared to be a deceivingly gentle current running through the floodwater, which was running directly towards the depths of the river, gradually increasing in strength and speed. The rain blurred my vision from under the dripping hood of my anorak, but nevertheless, I finally reached my destination.

I didn't know how deep the water was around the house, but it was half way up the door, and there were steps leading up to that door. Believe it or not, I had never counted how many steps in all the years I had worked there. The water was far too murky to see the bottom, and I was afraid. I shouted up at the bedroom windows, where I was sure the Cheswicks would be if they had remained in the house. There was no answer, and no faces appeared at the window. I floated as near as I could to the windows, and then I saw the notice stuck to it from inside. It was a council notice informing the rescue services that the house had been successfully evacuated. I felt relieved.

I paddled my makeshift raft around to the back of the house so I could look over as much of the fields as I could. Those fields were very important to me. There was a part of me in every one of them; I loved them, in fact.

I could just make out the grove of trees that separated the northern fields from the southern. There were some odd shapes floating amongst the trees, perhaps debris of some kind. I wasn't sure, but they could even be animals, even worse, they could be bodies. I was horrified. What if they were dead bodies, corpses! I had to get down there—pronto.

I maneuvered the table so it was pointing towards the southern field and paddled towards the grove of trees. It was then that I realized my mistake. The current had got stronger, and I found that I couldn't back-paddle strongly enough to escape it. I was heading towards the river. I started to panic and paddled desperately towards the grove.

Thankfully, I saw that I was finally being drawn towards the grove of trees, and I relaxed and let the waters take me there. I was back in my childhood self, back in the wardrobe, back in the running, overwhelming flood water of my dreams. And it was in this dreamlike state that I saw that the shapes were, indeed, bodies. Or what remained of them.

The water slowed around the tree, and there they all were in this sacred burial ground. There was Marisol, still in her white nightgown, lying face upwards amongst the weeds like Millais's *Ophelia*. She had risen from her grave along with the others.

There were Sharon's decomposed remains and the more recent Jacky, bloated as if the water had swollen her corpse into a horribly lifelike swimming aid.

There were many others, their strangled bodies floating like so many awful, ruined lilies, some now just mere skeletons with tattered rags hanging off them. It seemed as though their bony arms reached out to me as if beseeching me to restore the life I had taken.

I knew I could not go back now. There was no place to go back to. I let the river's current take me where it would, faster now, faster through the running dark waters, streaming back on this false flood tide, back to my beginning.

CHRISTMAS AT AUSCHWITZ

The Kommandant scrutinized himself in the bathroom mirror. He was, as usual, impeccably shaven and brushed, and his pitch-black SS uniform was immaculately pressed. The way the death's head insignias on his uniform and hat glittered particularly pleased him. He must remember to give his butler a little bonus for Christmas.

He looked in on his wife in their bedroom before he went downstairs. She was sleeping peacefully, making those little snoring noises he found so endearing. But the children were already up. He could hear them giggling with excitement. No doubt they were already gathered around the candlelit Christmas tree, opening their presents. He could hear the rustling and tearing of paper being ripped off carefully wrapped presents and the little gasps of delight as each fresh discovery was made. He decided he would also leave them in peace; there would be plenty of time for him to join in the family festivities when he returned in the afternoon.

His chauffeur was waiting for him outside, standing at rigid attention alongside the heavy black Mercedes. The Kommandant looked up into the sky. It was pure white. There would be even heavier snowfall today. No doubt his four elder children would build an enormous snowman as they had been longing to do all winter.

He looked into the distance where the twin chimneys of Auschwitz dominated the skyline. They were both churning out streams of steady black smoke, but it was not the amount of smoke the Kommandant wished to see. He wanted veritable clouds of smoke billowing into the skies. He would soon see to that. He had a special Christmas treat lined up for the Jewish scum: there were to be double shifts at the gas chambers and crematoria today.

He ordered his chauffeur to put on the radio. There would be many jolly Christmas songs today. He was particularly looking forward to the Führer's speech, which was to be broadcast in the early evening. He tapped his feet along with "Jingle Bells." Although not strictly a Germanic tune, it was catchy, nevertheless. It put one in the right Christmas spirit, he thought.

The Kommandant skimmed through the papers on his desk. They had a cargo of over one thousand arriving that very morning. He had ordered the SS guards to be especially dutiful and swift in their duties. The selection process was to be double quick, only the very fittest for the work camps. The rest were to be exterminated immediately. Meanwhile, the backlog was to be dealt with. He would have those furnaces burning red hot today, as hot as the fires of Hell, where all of the enemies of Christendom belonged. He decided he would visit the train stop himself. It would inspire his SS guards to be more ruthless than ever.

The huge train ground to a halt accompanied by its raucous whistles. Floodlights drenched the train in unnaturally bright light. The dogs kept on tight leashes were now allowed to bark and bare their fangs—they knew what was coming.

The Kommandant had ordered them starved for two days, so they were in a particularly vicious mood, snarling and yelping in anticipation of anything or anyone they could attack.

The heavy freight doors of the train were thrown open. Its occupants blinked at the sudden, intense light and noise. They cowered back, but the soldiers were already pulling them out of the freights carts. Older people stumbled and fell and were kicked until they got up. The female SS guards ripped babies from their mother's arms and either dashed their brains out against the brick walls or fed them to the dogs. Everything was accompanied by the words "*schnell, schnell*," quick, quick. The Jews were so dazed by what was happening they hardly knew it when they were marched straight off to the shower rooms. The Kommandant noted with satisfaction that his orders were being carried out to the letter: spare no one, show no mercy. The moans of the prisoners were replaced by wailing and screams. And it was constant. Screams of agony and pain mixed with sobbing and cries of anguish. The Kommandant looked at the pitiful Jews as they were marched to the gas chambers. Some knew what to expect and hung their heads in submission. Others thought they were really going to have just a shower. The reception they received swiftly disillusioned them of that dream.

The Kommandant watched in silent approval as two SS guards kicked an old man to death. A young man, probably the old man's grandson, was being forcibly restrained. The Kommandant decided it was time for him to act, always good to set an example. He marched over to where the struggling young man was being held back by two SS privates and, without preamble, shot him in the temple with his Mauser. The two guards threw the corpse to some kapos who rushed off with it to the furnaces. The old man would soon join him. The Kommandant let his soldiers have their fun with him as the old man lay writhing on the ground in agony. Nothing like a bit of Jew-baiting to raise morale. He decided to pay a visit to the crematoria.

The furnaces were in full swing now. The kapos were loading in corpses every few minutes and stirring the "soup," as they called it—the fat from the burning corpses that was boiling and bubbling at the bottom of the ovens. He reprimanded an SS-Oberschütze who was reluctant to put a little girl in the ovens. She had somehow miraculously survived the gas chamber and was quite alive and crying out for her mother. The Kommandant ordered her thrown in alive.

Back in his office, the Kommandant looked down the list of cargo due to arrive that day. With any luck, they should beat last year's record. The chimneys were now belching a thick fog of black smoke mixed with sparks. It was quite pretty, he thought, rather like a primitive fireworks display. He decided that enough was enough. He had done enough work for the day, it was time to return to his family; after all, it was Christmas.

As the car drew up in front of his house, he saw that his children, as expected, were making a large snowman. His second-youngest daughter, Inge, ran up to him as he got out of the Mercedes.

"Papa, there is something wrong with the snow."

He looked at her tiny hands. Usually immaculately clean, they were nearly black. His little one was right. There was something wrong with the snow. It was black, not white. The snowflakes that were falling were mixed with ash. He looked at his children's black hands; they were covered in the greasy muck. The falling snow had become mixed with falling ashes belched from the twin chimneys.

He ordered his children inside. He kicked angrily at the now—grey snow. Trust the filthy Jews. Even in death, they managed to spoil Christmas.

THE MYNAH BIRD

Dr. Jeremy B. Clarkson, M.D., D.O., glared at the caged bird. The psychiatrist had originally bought the accursed creature for his wife, but somehow it had ended up in his study.

He thought his wife would be happy with the present. She had, after all, professed an admiration of talking birds at a recent dinner party, a singular and revelatory fact of which he hitherto had been unaware. Armed with this surprising piece of information, he had bought her a mynah bird at a nearby pet shop.

This particular fact, like many uttered by his wife when she had consumed one glass of wine too many, had proved to be utterly false. Much to his frustration, not to mention cost, she had returned it to him, saying that she couldn't get the ridiculous thing to say a word.

"Damn it! Why don't you say something? I might as well have bought the proverbial dead parrot," he grumbled at the recalcitrant fowl

"At last, a show of emotion," the mynah bird drawled. "You do have them. You don't know how boring you psychiatrists can be. Sitting there analyzing everything but showing nothing."

Dr. Clarkson's jaw dropped so far it narrowly avoided the floor. "You can speak?"

"Is that a rhetorical question? Can I speak he, asks? It is self-evident I can speak, or we wouldn't be having this conversation. I only talk when I feel I can have a worthwhile conversation. Do you know how boring it is to have you humans constantly repeating the same words at me, as if I were some kind of senile, imbecilic budgerigar. You'll be chanting 'Pretty Polly' at me next. In fact, that's what your slut of a wife kept on repeating for days on end. I could have pecked her eyes out given half a chance."

"This is incredible!" the doctor exclaimed. He reached for his ever-present voice recorder.

"I really wouldn't do that," the mynah bird said. "I'll only clam up again, and then you'll look very foolish. This conversation, as regards third parties, is strictly between you and me."

"At least that clears something up—I'm not mad. Please, I implore you. Let me get my wife."

"The question of your sanity is, at the very best, debatable. But please don't get her. At least for the immediate future. Also, I can't abide the smell of a freshly fucked cunt. I'm surprised you can stand it without throwing up, speaking for myself, of course."

"What do you mean freshly fucked?" Dr. Clarkson's face reddened in embarrassment at the use of the word, plus the sudden exit of all Wodehousian polite discourse, mixed with a trace of indignation and a large dollop of disbelief that he was carrying on a conversation with a bird, and on top of all that, a conversation about sexual matters—intimate particulars concerning him and his spouse, which would be embarrassing for any husband. Notwithstanding the aforementioned, there was the obvious incongruity and irony of a psychiatrist confessing to a mynah bird. He lurched on regardless.

"We haven't, ahem, indulged in copulation for several months."

He felt his face flushing despite himself. This was ridiculous!

"Indulged in copulation...Who the hell talks like that? Listen to yourself," the bird said, mimicking Dr. Clarkson's whiny, slightly defensive tone exactly. "You sound like an encyclopedia. No wonder she's fucking the guy next door every opportunity she gets."

"You mean than unemployed layabout who spends all his time tinkering with his filthy motorbike?"

"The one and only. Haven't you noticed the grease marks on her fat arse? He's not just been riding his fucking bike. I told you, psychiatrists are blind to what's in front of their eyes because their brains are too busy analyzing inconsequential crap. Ring a bell?"

Dr. Clarkson stifled an indignant reply. Was he, a trained psychiatrist, going insane? He was sure mynah birds were not capable of this level of communication. He had checked up on them on Wikipedia before he went to the pet store. They were just clever mimics, like parrots. There were unconfirmed rumors, however, that they deliberately imitated other birds for their own gain, which would signify a very high level of intelligence, indeed. No! He must be having some kind of psychotic episode. He needed help, but he was loath to contact any of his peers. If word should get out...

The bird seemed to read his thoughts.

"If you think you're non compos mentis, you're not. See for yourself—go find your wife. I bet she's in the bathroom right now flushing out her dirty old hole. She didn't pop to the shops like she told you half an hour ago. She was having a quickie in his garage, doggy style, apparently. They do say in that position you get maximum penetration, and his load would have been right up her. I heard her planning it with him on the telephone last night, right here in your study, whilst you were having a bath. They like talking about the act in detail before they do it. Well, they do say anticipation is nine-tenths of delight."

Dr. Clarkson bit his tongue to stop himself from losing his temper. This really was intolerable. First, he'd bought a mynah bird that refused to talk. Now it wouldn't shut up. On top of that, the bird only seemed able to utter obscenities and vile accusations against his spouse. He had, however, long suspected his wife of having an affair. But having a feathered mammal, and a sub-species at that, point it out to him really was the limit. He charged out of the room, yelling for his wife.

"Patricia!"

A mumbled reply came from the upstairs bathroom, along with the sound of a running tap.

"Just coming, Jeremy."

He was sure he had detected a slight giggle in her voice when she had said "coming," a word she had enunciated with unwarranted emphasis, he thought; at the same time, he was desperately trying to decide if he was becoming paranoid. His wife rarely giggled. He was almost certainly sure she had never done so in front of him, anyway. The sound of running water ceased. She emerged from the bathroom—in her bathrobe!

"I thought you were going to the shops," he said, trying to make his whiny voice less whiny.

"I've been," she said, smiling at him as she came down the stairs. "But I felt so sweaty afterwards I thought I'd have a quick freshen-up. What's the matter?"

Dr. Clarkson's face had noticeably reddened.

"Yes, it is rather humid. I think I'll give my face a quick splash as well."

His wife gave him a strange look as he hurriedly brushed past her on his way up to the bathroom. Sure enough, the large towel and the hand towel were wet. But there was also a pair of wet knickers, freshly rinsed if he wasn't mistaken, hanging over the shower taps. His wife's other clothes were in the laundry basket. He checked them for oil stains.

He caught a glimpse of himself in the mirror. His wispy grey hair was in disarray, and his eyes looked large, red, and swollen through his steel-rimmed glasses. He took a deep breath, washed his face, straightened his tie, pulled his beige cardigan straight, and combed his thinning hair into a well-practiced comb-over. Satisfied that he looked more presentable and that he had recovered his equanimity, he returned downstairs.

"Patricia, why are there a pair of your knickers hanging over the shower taps? It's most unsightly!"

"I gave them a quick rinse. I really was sooo sweaty. They're nylon. They'll dry in no time." She gave him a scathing look. "Since when have you been interested in my knickers, anyway?" she said with a bitter laugh. "The only time they ever get wet is when I run them under the tap!"

Dr. Clarkson was not going to allow himself to be drawn into an argument. He could guess what kind of crude vocabulary his wife would start using next. No doubt, there would be many references to the size of his penis and its unfortunate state of permanent flaccidity. He simply ignored the crude statement, pecked her on the cheek, picked up his briefcase, and went to work. Later, whilst her erstwhile husband was at work, Patricia phoned their next-door neighbor from the study.

"I think he's on to us, Geoff. He was acting really peculiar this morning. Yes, I know, honey. I'm dying for it again, too, but you know old Miss Simmonds is always out in her garden in the afternoons—it's too risky. We'll have to cool it for a couple of days. I'm sorry. I wish I could suck it better, too. I know, why don't we meet up at Ellington Park on Wednesday morning? Limp dick's got a surgery. We can have a good shag in the back of your van. I'll make it up to you. Yeah, up my arse and everything. Make it half past ten. I know, I can't wait either. Keep it nice and hard for me."

A succession of kisses followed, and some throaty grunts of satisfaction. Mrs. Clarkson paid no heed to the mynah bird ruffling its feathers and shaking its head, or the little pile of vomit at the bottom of its cage.

Once Mrs. Clarkson had left her husband's study, the mynah bird's behavior changed extraordinarily. It hopped over to the cage's door. Carefully clutching one of the rungs and balancing on one of its legs, it put the other through the bars of the cage and delicately lifted the latch. It hopped, some of the anthropomorphic persuasion might say, with glee, over to the recently used telephone. It pecked redial. At the other end, Geoff picked up.

"It's me again," the mynah bird said in a perfect imitation of Patricia Clarkson's voice. "About Wednesday, make sure you bring one of your big tools—no, not that one, silly." (The bird executed a passable snorting chuckle). "A big wrench. Don't worry what for...It'll be for something that'll feel good, I promise."

The mynah bird did some suitable girly giggling, and pressed the red hook button.

It tapped out the code for untraceable calls and phoned Dr. Clarkson's mobile. An irritated, short-tempered Dr. Clarkson answered, "Who is this? How did you get my number."

"Never mind the how and who. All you need to know is that I have some very useful information to impart to you."

The mynah bird was using a very authoritative, masculine voice, which the bird knew would wrong-foot the doctor.

"If you're selling something, I 'm not buying," Dr. Clarkson said, trying his best to sound in control. It had been a very stressful morning, and he did not feel like talking to complete strangers. After all, it was his mobile. But the voice somehow reminded him of his father—that quiet authority. He would have immediately recognized, if he had made a self-diagnosis, that he had automatically gone into a submissive role.

"Stop wasting my time and listen," the voice commanded. "Your wife and her lover, not content with making you a pitiful cuckold, are planning to kill you. If you want to see the evidence with your own eyes, go to Ellington Park car park at half past ten on Wednesday morning. And make sure you have a weapon of some sort."

"But..." Dr. Clarkson was about to protest, but the line had gone dead. He checked for a number. As he thought: WITHELD. He had been about to tell the telephonic intruder in his workspace that he would be working on that particular date. Then it struck him. If his wife did want to meet someone, which he did not believe for a moment, to discuss how they might murder him, then Wednesday at half past ten was the perfect time to do it.

It would not do to the let a client down by going on some wild goose chase just because of a strange, anonymous phone call. But all things considered...today had been pretty strange altogether. Perhaps he should also explore the possibilities that this might really be a psychotic episode. Had he imagined the phone call? If he really wanted to test his sanity, then the only way to do it was to physically investigate the situation before it got any worse.

He pressed the intercom to his secretary and told her to rearrange his Wednesday morning. Ms. Walker made no comment even though Dr. Clarkson never missed or changed appointments. Quiet and faithfully efficient, just the way he liked a secretary to be.

Mrs. Clarkson had once been his secretary, and a pretty good one, he thought. But that had been years ago because he had made the very unfortunate and unretractable mistake of marrying her. Although, anyone would think from her continual moaning that she had been the one who had made the mistake. The problems, or more accurately, the problem, had started some years ago, in fact, more years than he liked to remember, and had been there even before he'd got married. It was a diagnosed medical disorder, he repeatedly pointed out to his wife, common to many men of his age. ED, or erectile dysfunction, was only natural with age. She always managed to counter with the fact that he couldn't even get it up with Viagra, and that wasn't normal. This was incontrovertibly true. Even the little blue pills did not manage to stir his stubbornly, permanently flaccid member.

He had tried everything, from yoga to acupuncture to every kind of vitamin supplement imaginable, and he'd read voraciously on the subject, but theory and practice stubbornly refused to get along. It was age and stress, he had decided. Completely normal. The fact that the actual physical act of copulation was somewhat abhorrent to him had nothing to do with it—Dr. Clarkson firmly believed that. He had performed a self- diagnosis on himself and found that nothing was wrong with him.

The fault obviously lay with his oversexed wife. She had her consolations. They lived in a smart detached house in a select neighborhood. He had bought her a brand-new sports car. They eat out every Friday night. He had even bought her the rubber thing for her other needs. He had seen to that as well; after all, he was the one always buying batteries for the hideous device. She insisted he buy them to make him feel guilty. That was another thing, he thought with a frown. She hadn't asked for more batteries since the Neanderthal next door had moved in. His furrowed brow furrowed some more. Mere coincidence? He was starting to sweat as he thought about the large life insurance policy he had taken out. They had no children, of course; Mrs. Clarkson was the sole beneficiary.

Wednesday morning, Dr. Clarkson went off to work as usual. His wife had seemed her usual sarcastic self. Any remark he made was met with some acerbic comment. Things couldn't have been more normal. The mynah bird had refused to say another word since the episode. Dr Clarkson was sure that when he investigated the Ellington Park business, it would all prove to be a hoax or prank in bad taste, or perhaps even mild hallucinations brought on by overwork. His wife was always complaining that it was always work, work, work with him, that they should have more leisure time to spend enjoying themselves. He would cut down next year, he decided. Then he could dedicate more time to his begonias.

He pictured his wife in a hat and sunglasses, lounging in a deckchair, sipping a glass of cool lemonade, watching him contentedly whilst he tended the flowers. A very pleasant, almost rural scene. They both would thoroughly enjoy that, he decided. Who needed so-called exciting, exotic holidays when they had bliss right there in their back garden amidst the perennial borders?

Dr. Clarkson arrived at Ellington Park sometime before half past ten, but it was not by car. He had driven into town and, from there, taken a taxi. He wandered aimlessly through the trees surrounding the car park, to all intents and purposes just another casual park-goer taking a stroll. In reality, Dr. Clarkson, who had taken the precaution of wearing an anorak, a woolen beanie hat, and a different pair of spectacles he had bought in town, was keeping a very sharp eye on the car park. Not that there was much to keep an eye on. Ellington Park was not that popular. It was mostly frequented by drunks and junkies who would have been incapable of driving a vehicle anyway, even if they could have afforded one.

The more Dr. Clarkson wandered about trying to look innocuous, the more conspicuous he felt. He remembered the "weapon" in his briefcase. Things would look even more suspicious if he was stopped and, for some reason, searched by the police.

The weapon in question was the only thing that Dr. Clarkson had managed to find in his house that was not either lethal or, on the other hand, useless. He could not take a kitchen knife or hammer, and one of his large medical tomes, although heavy, would need both hands to wield. He had finally remembered his wife's scary collection of sex toys. He rummaged in her wardrobe and, in triumph, found a huge black rubber dildo. It was solid and heavy and would make an excellent cosh if need be.

He now sincerely regretted his choice and put it down to another sign of the fragility of his state of mind. He was now desperately looking for somewhere to dispose of the hideous thing, but it was just then that his wife chose to drive through the gates.

Patricia had arrived exactly on time in her little red sports car. For some strange reason, her promptness gave Dr. Clarkson a feeling of almost solicitous pride. His wife was punctual, but trust the greasy gorilla to be late. Thoughts of the impending arrival of his nemesis sobered the doctor. It was true, then. It had never been a prank or psychotic episode. His mind frantically searched for other reasons his wife might be there: perhaps she really did have a deep-seated interest in ornithology and she was there to do some bird watching, or maybe she was going to take a nice stroll. Just then, his mobile vibrated. He swore under his breath and then saw it was a WITHELD number. He pressed the receiver button.

"Are you there at the location you were informed about?" It was the same mysterious, authoritative voice.

"Yes," he replied.

"Remember what I told you. They are planning to kill you. Have you got a voice recorder with you?"

"Yes. I never go anywhere without it."

"I know," the voice said mysteriously. Dr. Clarkson wanted to ask how he knew, but he sensed there wasn't enough time and he wouldn't get an answer anyway.

"Get in close, photograph and record them. Then you'll have all the proof you need. You can go to the police if you like, but either way, you'll be holding all the trumps."

Dr. Clarkson nodded instinctively, even though he was on the phone. He liked playing whist. Perhaps that was something he could do with Patricia when all this had blown over. A little harmless excitement would do her good. They could even play knockout whist for money! Just for pennies, though, he admonished himself. It wouldn't do to get carried away.

"Make sure you've got your weapon handy," the voice continued, bringing him back down to earth.

Dr. Clarkson still didn't understand why he should need a weapon; he was not a man of violence. But he had trusted the voice up to now and in for a penny, in for a pound...

It was then that the gorilla drew up in the large, dark blue Transit van that he used to take his motorbike to races. He parked next to his wife's trendy little car. Dr. Clarkson hid behind the tree and took photos with his mobile; unfortunately, these later proved to be selfies. His heart was racing. He took the dildo out of his briefcase. It felt heavier in his hands than it had in the briefcase, and its black menace, the doctor realized, looked surprisingly intimidating, at least to him. Dr. Clarkson now congratulated himself on his ingenuity and returned to his hiding place behind the tree with the improvised cosh. Geoff was out of the Transit and chatting to his wife. They were going to the back of the van. Dr. Clarkson used his mobile to take some more quick photos as they disappeared into its windowless interior. At least he had some evidence now. What he really wanted was concrete evidence of the plot to murder him. The anonymous informer was right—he needed verbal evidence as well as visual.

He stealthily approached the windowless rear doors of the van. He came at the doors from the side. One of the back doors was slightly ajar. The lazy Neanderthal hadn't even bothered to close it properly. Typical! But he had to admit, it was just right for listening.

He put his head close to the gap and slid the recording device in between the door. There didn't seem to be much talking going on—just a lot of rustling and moaning. Was his wife in pain? Was the filthy wretch performing some kind of Hells Angels' sadistic sexual act on her? Why couldn't his wife, if she had chosen to be unfaithful, be intimate with a normal, respectable person? He risked opening the door, just enough, so he could take a surreptitious peep inside.

Even through that thin space, the stench and sound of sexual intercourse hit him like a punch in the stomach. The distinctive, long-forgotten smell of his wife's vagina mixed with her favorite perfume, the smell of oil, and the gorilla Geoff's awful sweat made him gag. In the gloom, he could just make out a pair of hairy buttocks pounding up and down between a pair of fish-stockinged legs, held high by his wife's long, ring-covered fingers. She was moaning as if in pain, gasping terrible sexual obscenities that he had not thought her capable of, or indeed, any person. Her short skirt was pulled up around her waist. A pair of small red lace knickers were hanging off one of her ankles, dancing in time to the pounding between her legs. She was still wearing her high heels.

For some bizarre reason, he had to see her face just to make sure it was her, though of course he knew it was. Dr. Clarkson decided that both of them were too far gone in their throes of sexual congress to notice him climbing inside. He had to see her face, even though he could clearly hear that it was her voice uttering those gross, crude words. He had to see it. For an instant, he caught a glimpse of it over the burly brute's shoulder. His hairy anus was pumping up and down on her, deep, thrusts that slapped wetly against her thighs like meat being slammed onto a butcher's slab. His wife's eyes were screwed shut, her mouth twisted in a rictus of sensual pleasure. The contorted face was a picture of pure delight. The gorilla's grunting was increasing in volume.

His wife's crimson-painted nails were now digging tightly into the pounding buttocks, holding them on her in a writhing frenzy.

"That's it, Geoff, fill my hole with cum!" squealed Patricia Clarkson.

Dr. Clarkson watched in revulsion as she clutched the monster's hairy buttocks even more feverishly as they both prepared for their mutual orgasms. They both cried out in unison, which seemed to last for an eternity. But then it stopped. And his wife opened her eyes! Her first reaction was baffled amazement as she caught sight of her slack-jawed husband's head, topped by a strange, garish woolly hat, peering at her over Geoff's shoulder. Then she screamed...

Dr. Clarkson hastily tried to retreat out of the back of the van on his hands and knees, but his stupid anorak was snagged on something. He beat at the something with the dildo. His mobile phone and recorder went sliding across the metal floor of the van.

"What the fuck!" Geoff said, rolling off Mrs. Clarkson and pulling up his jeans.

Patricia Clarkson looked at the phone and recorder.

"The filthy pervert was trying to film us." She glared at her kneeling husband. "You really are beyond disgusting!" She skewered the recorder with a well-aimed kick of her stiletto.

"Me, disgusting...!" Dr. Clarkson, spluttered indignantly, waving the black dildo much like the caveman waving a bone at the beginning of *2001: A Space Odyssey*. Ironically, it was the very picture he had in mind when he thought of Geoff, the other male occupant of the van. If he hadn't been confined by its spatial limitations, he would have hopped up and down in speechless rage.

"Look out, he's got a weapon!" Mrs. Clarkson screamed as she scrambled to the back of the van, pulling up her knickers. "He's gone mad!" It was then that she saw what her husband was clutching, and burst into hysterical laughter. "Don't worry, even that's gone floppy on him. What you going to do with it, Mr. Floppy, shove it up Geoff's arse? I bet you'd like that. I always knew you were a filthy pervert."

Whilst it was true that Dr. Clarkson had a wild look in his bespectacled eyes and was spluttering so much he was beginning to foam at the mouth as if had momentarily contracted an unfortunate case of rabies, he was not insane or perverted; he could have told them that—he was a professional in the field of what constituted sanity. In fact, he thought he was behaving with remarkable dignity considering the circumstances.

The Neanderthal Geoff was eyeing him with evil intent, his hairy face screwed up in angry confusion and his beady eyes narrowed in crimson hatred. He picked up the wrench which he had been asked to bring and which they had not got around to using. The doctor backed away on his knees, clutching the dildo in front of him.

"Now, just you listen here. Don't you try anything. I'm warning you!" he said.

Dr. Clarkson waved the dildo menacingly in front of him. Unfortunately, his anorak chose that moment to un-snag itself, and he was catapulted head forward. And even more unfortunately, at that particular moment, Geoff chose to brandish the giant wrench. There was an unfortunate collision...

The pet shopkeeper put down the local newspaper, very reluctantly, at the sound of the shop door's buzzer. He had been in engrossed in the bizarre story of marital infidelity, sexual depravity, ménage à trois, and murder that had taken place right here in their very own town. It was front-page news.

Coincidentally, the murdered man had recently been a customer at the very same shop, and the man held on suspicion of murder was the man's next-door neighbor, who had been bonking the man's wife, apparently aided by the murdered doctor with a sex toy. Things had got out of hand as they often do in those kinds of situations. A veritable web of vice and intrigue.

The shopkeeper did not appear to be in the least surprised when he looked up and saw the uniformed policeman carrying a bird cage containing a mynah bird.

"I believe this is yours, sir." The policeman nodded at the newspaper's front page. "Mrs. Clarkson said her late husband bought it here and she no longer wants it. She asked us to return it to you." He placed the cage on the counter.

As soon as the policeman had left, the shopkeeper said, "That one didn't take you long. Front-page news!"

"You owe me one female mynah bird," said the mynah bird.

"I always pay my bets. You know that," the shopkeeper said as he went out to the back room.

He returned with another mynah bird in a cage. He placed the cage next to the other one.

"A fledging, just like you like 'em. I've put plenty of hemp in her bird seed, so she's flying high as a kite," the shopkeeper said.

"Perfect," replied the mynah bird. "But next time, I choose the mark. Someone who presents a bit more of a challenge..."

THE TOKEN

I suppose it was out of sheer boredom that I walked into the charity shop. I only usually go into them to buy the odd second-hand book or two, and I really had enough reading material at home to keep me going for quite a while. There was the usual mix of books that I had either read before or immediately knew I would not enjoy. But there were a couple of hardbacks that caught my eye, and as the outlay for both was £2.00, I decided it was well within my budget.

There was a kindly-looking old gentleman behind the counter who was struggling to manage the mechanics of the electric till. While he struggled, I had a glance at the little glass counter that lay in front.

For quite a number of years, I had avoided buying anything that appeared to be antique or valuable. It seemed that everybody now thought their pieces of junk were worth a fortune, due, I suppose, to all the television programs that seemed to have caught peoples' imagination. I sometimes felt like pointing out that I could buy exactly the same shirt or piece of china brand new for less than the price that they were selling it at.

Something caught my eye, though. It was what looked like a silver coin of some sort. Unfortunately, someone had drilled a hole through the top, presumably for a necklace or bracelet. The inscriptions were what more intrigued me, though. Judging by the symbols, they looked to be Asian of some kind.

The old man had finished dithering with the till, and I handed over the two pound coins. Out of curiosity, I asked to look at the ruined coin.

"I've often wondered about it myself," he said. "It's Chinese, I think, and was probably a good luck charm of some sort. But the other side is blank, so I think it may have just been unfinished and thrown away. The symbols on the front, I believe, are meant to represent good luck. You know how much the Chinese believe in good luck." He winked at me.

I would not usually waste my limited financial resources on trinkets, but there was something about the charm, or good luck token, or whatever it was, that fascinated me, and I also knew it would fit perfectly on an old silver bracelet I wore. I asked the price.

The old man picked it out of the glass case gingerly, as if it were something precious, and, putting on a pair of quite extraordinarily large spectacles, looked at the small price tag.

"Just two pounds, sir. I daresay it's not a bad price for a piece of luck."

He gave me a shy, sardonic smile.

I am pragmatic at the best of times, and today I was going to give my mother the usual weekly bunch of flowers, which would cost exactly that amount. But I knew she wouldn't even notice them if I brought them or not, as she had been senile for a number of years now. So, I bought it there and then on the spur of the moment.

It fitted smoothly and beautifully onto my bracelet, and it was with a strange kind of satisfaction that I left the shop. The old man had removed his spectacles, and I noticed he had the clearest green eyes I had ever seen, except perhaps on a cat. They shone like emeralds.

When I got home, there was the usual stack of letters on the doormat: junk mail, bills—all the usual stuff.

"Anything in the post for me!" my mother shouted down from her bedroom, where she spent the majority of her time.

She might have been going senile, but her hearing was still excellent. And the post was one of the highlights of her day even though there was hardly ever anything for her.

"Fraid not, Mum. I'll bring you up a cuppa in a minute."

I sensed her usual disappointment. Despite not having received any mail for years, she still lived in hope that someone out there would remember her when her wits were about her.

Whilst drinking my tea, I sorted through the mail. Most of it went in the bin. A pink envelope caught my eye. It turned out to be from the premium bonds, no doubt my latest statement as I had recently withdrawn another hundred, leaving me with the bare minimum. I always liked to have a bit of hope of winning something, though, so I hadn't taken out everything.

As I read its contents, I spilled half of my tea on my lap. I had won! I had actually won! And not just one of the little wins you get every few years or so. It was the jackpot! A million quid. I was actually a genuine millionaire.

I checked the letter over again thoroughly. There are so many scams nowadays I felt that it might be just another one. The more I read it, the more convinced I was that it was a trick of some kind. I rang the number. It was really from NS&I, and I had won.

I ran upstairs to tell Mum the news and found her in a remarkably cheerful mood as if she had somehow already known. But for a change, she seemed to just be in a happy mood. What was even stranger: she didn't even seem to be excited that much by my huge good fortune. She usually got excited if people were excited around her, which, admittedly, was rare nowadays. Was it another form of her senility? She seemed perfectly calm and in control of herself like she had been in her prime.

"Do you know, dear, I really am feeling much better today. Don't know why—must be the weather."

I was tempted to disagree as it was wet and miserable outside, but I didn't want to spoil her mood, for however long it might last.

"All that money, darling. Think of all the things you could do with it, go on holiday, see the world, get a nice car."

I was about to mention that she knew full well that I had failed my test six times now, but then I thought better of it; she seemed in such a radiant mood.

I would have to give serious consideration as to what I would do with the money. Going abroad was out of the question given mum's condition, although I had always fancied travelling. Surprisingly enough, it was she who came up with a solution.

"I could have a carer in while you're away, son, and she would be here twenty-four hours so you wouldn't have to worry. You need a break. You've been so good to me over all these years, and you can send me some lovely postcards."

I was astounded. They were the most sensible words she had spoken to me for years.

I thought about it all day at work. I had never been abroad. The only travelling I had ever done was the occasional caravan trip around England, when my dad was alive, and to be honest, I was a bit scared of going to another country by myself. I was also scared of the huge amount of money I had come into. I've been a bachelor all my life, and my job and looking after Mum basically summed up my life. I didn't like change; even my various dalliances with the opposite sex had all been embarrassing failures. I was simply too shy and staid in my ways.

Miss Eddison came into my office with papers from the account's department. She was no doubt the most attractive female in the firm and no doubt was quite aware of it. So many of my colleagues lusted after her and made no secret of it, but she was in a league of her own and knew it. She looked at me and gave me a cheerful smile.

"You look glum today, Mr. Thompson. What's the matter, your mum doing poorly again?"

I couldn't help but tell her the truth and my dilemma. She gave me one of her dazzling smiles.

"You are silly. Your mum's right: you need a break. Wow! With all that money, you should be drinking Champagne, not tea. If I'm not being too forward—I could be your companion abroad. I have travelled quite a lot. Not that you need a companion, of course. I'm sure you would be able to take care of yourself perfectly well.

"And there's so much to see out there. I'll bring you some brochures later, and you can decide on somewhere, and if you want me to come along, you only have to ask." She beamed at me once more and left.

She did as promised, and we spent the best part of the afternoon looking at exotic travel destinations. The prices were mind-boggling, but now I realized I could afford it. I had to adjust to my new financial position.

In the end, we settled on Mexico, and I say *we* because she agreed to come along and could also speak a bit of Spanish. She made the arrangements the very next day. I glanced over them and noted there was only one room booked for the two of us—a luxury double.

"But what about you?" I asked.

"Don't be silly," she said. "We'll share the same bed. I'll be wearing pyjamas, and I promise I won't get up to anything naughty. That's if you don't." She giggled.

I was still in a daze when I arrived home. Not only was I a millionaire, but suddenly I was off to Mexico with the female of my dreams. So, it really it came as no surprise to find my mother was up and about and had actually prepared the evening meal herself. And considering she had been bedridden for God knows how many years it should have been something of a miracle. But I was really in too much of a kind of dream caused by the recent events to take it all in.

"It's only shepherd's pie, but I know that's one of your favorites. I don't know what's got into me today. I feel ten years younger."

She even did a little waltz around the table.

The carer was arranged, although, when she arrived, she seemed dubious of the fact that my mother needed looking after at all. She was up and about like my mum of old. But I insisted.

The taxi to the airport arrived on time, and I picked up Sheila, as she now wanted me to call her.

"If we're going to go on holiday together, we should be calling each other by our first names, don't you think, Richard? Otherwise, it will be like some kind of business trip."

She gave me a peck on the cheek and we were on our way.

It was on the M25 that disaster struck. There had been some kind of pileup, and the traffic jam extended for miles. We both looked sullenly at our watches as the minutes ticked by and Mexico got further and further distant. We finally arrived at Heathrow, but it was two hours too late. The flight had long since left.

"Don't worry; you had insurance on it, so you'll get your money back. Are you sure there isn't somewhere else you would like to go?" Sheila asked as we dejectedly made our way home.

She cuddled up to me which was rather disconcerting but nice all the same.

"China," I said decisively. "I've always dreamed of going to China."

Her face lit up.

"Don't worry, I can arrange that. Any particular place?"

"China. It has to be Xion," I said, decisively. "I've always wanted to see the terracotta army."

"So have I! How wonderful. You see, it may not be as bad as you think. If we had just wanted to lie in the sun, we could have gone to Spain, not Mexico. China will be far more interesting—for both of us."

She snuggled closer.

It was all arranged very efficiently by Sheila in two days, and we were off again—except, this time, my mother was out in the front garden, waving us goodbye. The carer stood in the front door with her arms folded. My mother's health had improved so dramatically I knew I would need to get the doctor to examine her when I came back to find out just what was going on.

This time, we arrived perfectly in time, and sitting comfortably in our first-class seats we watched a couple of films, read whatever we were reading at the time, and dozed off in between.

We were met on arrival by our guide, an extremely nice young man, recently graduated in English, and very knowledgeable about the terracotta army. I was fascinated, but somehow I felt that Sheila was bored.

"Can't wait to get to the hotel," she kept whispering in my ear.

When we did, she practically ripped my clothes off, and before I knew it, I had just made love to a woman who would make centre-folds look like mere Page 3 girls.

We had a splendid dinner, and I suggested that the next day, instead of visiting the terracotta army site again we should ask our guide to show us some bits of the China of old, before it was all swept away by Mao, and we could also shop around and see if we could find anything interesting. Sheila was enthused with the idea.

So, the next morning, we found ourselves in the strange back alleys and markets where most of the Chinese do their bargaining, or some would say bartering or even shortchanging.

"There aren't many really good clothes shops," Sheila said. She was looking disdainfully at some cheap silk blouses.

So, I promised her that the next day, we would get our guide to take us to the best clothes shops. She was cheered no end and grabbed my arm closely.

"And I hear they have some lovely jewelry."

"We'll have a look at that as well," I promised.

It was while we were walking past one of the many market kiosks that had golden pork hocks, skewered and dripping juices and making my mouth water, that I saw opposite a strange little shop in the reflection of its steamy window. It wasn't what you would call antiquarian, as it seemed to sell all kinds of odds and ends, but all of it was long out of date. I suppose it was stuff we would call bric-a-brac. I suggested we have a nose around inside.

"If you don't mind, darling, I'll just sit and have a coffee." She had spotted just opposite one of the many chains of coffee shops that seem to spring up like weeds in the unlikeliest places.

In a way, I was glad. I knew it wasn't her kind of thing. I was the one for second-hand shops. She really only liked things that had a designer label on them.

The interior of the shop was murky and full of strange and familiar objects: transistor radios, gramophone sets, Bakelite telephones, Chinese vases cracked from so much use, tea-pots of all kinds of designs. The deeper I got into the shop, the murkier it became as if the objects blended into a mass of past remnants. It was only right at the back that I noticed the old lady sitting there, motionless, but with the gleaming green eyes of a cat.

To my surprise, she spoke excellent English, albeit with a familiar Chinese accent. She asked me if I was looking for something special.

"Nothing, really. I'm just browsing."

She nodded slightly.

I noticed a glass cabinet full of odd trinkets. And I suddenly remembered the token on my bracelet.

"Oh, perhaps you could help me out and tell me what this means?" I said. I showed her the token on my bracelet. "I think it's Chinese, but no one really seems to know."

The old woman looked at me, aghast, as if she could not believe what I was showing her. Then she spoke in a horror-stricken voice.

"Get out of shop now. Never come back!"

She rose from her seat in great agitation, and for all her frailty, I could see that she wanted to literally throw me out the shop. I reached the doorway as quickly as I could, but I felt I had to say something.

"I'm sorry. I just wanted to know what it meant."

"Get out! And take that *thing* with you."

I left as politely as I could trying to do some kind of clumsy Chinese bow for any offence I might have caused. She slammed the door shut and I heard it being bolted from the inside.

I met Sheila in the coffee shop and told her what had happened. Much to my surprise, Sheila knew quite a lot about Chinese mythology and superstitions. She explained that at university, she had gone out with a Chinese student who would lend her Chinese books (translated, of course), like the *I-Ching* and the *Art of War* amongst others.

"I only recognize the central symbol; we would recognize it as the number eight. The Chinese place a lot of importance on numbers and dates. It's the sign of good fortune, but the others, I don't recognize. And I can't understand why the other side is blank. Very unusual. Perhaps it was just discarded at some time without being finished. Like the old man told you where you bought it."

"Strange, though, when you think about it. I've had a lot of good fortune lately," I said.

"You don't really believe in all that stuff, do you? I mean, you're not Chinese. It does look nice on your bracelet, though." She held my hand tenderly. "We've both had good luck, really. I never expected to be here with you."

By the time we got back to England, we were engaged. My mother, who seemed even more sprightly than before we left, was over the moon.

"It's just what you need, Richard—a nice woman to look after you."

"But what about you, Mum? Can you cope with just the carer, or do you want us to move in here with you?"

I found out that my mother had dispensed with the carer altogether. She now did everything herself, the shopping, cooking, housework; she had even started doing a bit of decorating and joined a yoga class. She was like a woman in her thirties instead of a pensioner in her seventies.

We decided that once Sheila and I were married, we would get a place nearby so I could visit every day. My mother was perfectly content with the arrangement.

The next months went by in a whirl. Before I knew it, I was married and we had both left our jobs. We got the house at a knock-down price, and I bought Sheila a cherry-red

BMW convertible as a wedding present. We also bought a semi-derelict building, which we converted into flats and which Sheila managed to acquire rich-enough tenants to pay for the outrageous prices she had decided we should charge.

Sheila became our mutual business manager as she was much better with money than me. We were now very comfortably well off. Sheila insisted on buying me a whole set of new clothes every few months, which, I must admit, I did feel rather smart in, and they nearly matched in elegance the new clothes and jewelry she selected for herself. I had even changed my old reliable watch for a top-of-the-range Rolex, which made me feel paranoid every time we went out, as I was sure someone would mug me as soon as they saw it. Sheila just shrugged.

"Don't worry, it's fully insured, and besides that, it's all been paid for out of the business account—all tax deductible, like everything. You know what a brilliant accountant we have."

Yes, I did. His name was Keith, and he had always spent a lot of time with Sheila working in the accounts department. It was only natural that he should work for us. An office was rented where they sorted out all our business affairs, which were now quite extensive. As for me, apart from visiting my mother, I didn't really have much to do. We had a cleaner who took care of the house, and most nights, we ate out, or I got takeaway if Sheila was working late with Keith.

I got a dog. Something I had always wanted. A lovely Golden Labrador puppy. Sheila wasn't keen but changed her mind when she saw the good taking it for long walks was doing me. I suppose it got me out of her hair.

Then the great day came when Sheila announced she was pregnant. It came both as a wonderful surprise and a bit of a shock, as, for quite a while, she had gone off sex and we'd rarely had intercourse, but I suppose it must have been on one of those rare occasions. Anyway, I was over the moon, and of course, so was my mother. She had always dreamed of having a grandchild. She even started knitting baby clothes straight away. Sheila's parents were both dead, and she had no siblings so you could say we were Sheila's family, now with an added member.

It was a week after Sheila's surprise announcement that I noticed something very odd had happened to the token on my bracelet. The blank side was now face up, and try as I might, I couldn't get it off the bracelet and put the decorated side up—all very strange.

To make matters worse, the dog was sick, and after taking it to the vet, I visited my mother, who seemed unusually agitated for a change.

"Richard, there's something I must tell you. I've taken to having late-night walks as I don't seem to need the amount of sleep I used to. It's the only thing that settles me. I went past your office, and the light was on..."

"Yes, Sheila put in another late shift, Mum. She works too hard. I've told her. She'll have to slow down soon...She's got the baby to think of."

"Will you let me finish," my mother said irritably. I felt quite hurt as Mum hadn't raised her voice to me since she had got better.

"The venetian blinds were half open, and I had a peep through the gaps, and I saw Keith and Sheila—"

Just then, the door-bell rang. It was Sheila. My mother clamped her jaw tightly shut and gave my wife a scathing look for some reason.

"Richard, there you are," Sheila said. "Have you forgotten we're supposed to be having dinner with the Goldmans tonight? I thought you'd be ready by now. You can't go dressed like that!"

She frowned at the jeans and sweatshirt I was wearing.

I admitted I had completely forgotten, and we hurried off. I promised Mum I'd be back tomorrow so we could chat again. She just nodded.

On the way to the Goldmans, I told Sheila about the dog and what the vet had said and the medicine I had to put in its food every day.

"I told you that dog is your damn business," Sheila snapped. "You should never have got it in the first place. I couldn't be less interested. We've got a baby on the way, if you haven't noticed."

Everyone seemed to be snapping at me. To change the subject, I told her about the strange conversation I'd had with my mother.

Sheila looked furious.

"What the hell is she doing snooping around our offices at that time of night, nosey parker. She's going doolally again!"

"She was only going for a walk. It just happened to be on the way. Anyway, she never got round to telling me whatever it was. I expect she'll tell me tomorrow."

Sheila frowned, and I decided to let the matter drop. I didn't want to spoil the evening, as I liked the Goldmans.

They were very hospitable hosts. Sometimes a little too hospitable when it came to wine, but it was always good stuff, and I suppose I drank quite a bit more than usual. It had been a stressful day. Sheila didn't even have one glass of wine, insisting that she didn't want to be caught drinking and driving and she had the baby to think of, although it had never bothered her before.

She didn't talk to me on the way back. She appeared to be deep in thought, probably something to do with business, I suppose, but I was too drunk to really care. When we got home, she insisted I have a hot drink as it would help with the inevitable hangover I was bound to be suffering from tomorrow. She could be so caring at times, even when she was in a bad mood. I forced it down, only just managing to remove my jacket before I fell onto the bed into a deep sleep

When I finally awoke, it had gone midday, and I felt awful. I didn't bother to even shave or change my clothes as the poor dog must have been dying to get out for a walk. I put on my jacket and noticed a dark stain on the sleeve. I must have spilt some wine on it at the Goldmans. Still, it was probably nothing that the dry-cleaners couldn't shift.

The dog, as I expected, was whining at the front door and leaped for joy when it saw me take down its lead. It did its business, and I cleaned it up, and then we headed for Mum's place. The fresh air was at least waking me up a bit.

I rang the bell. There was not the usual shout of "Just coming" I expected to hear, and the curtains were still drawn. I rang again and knocked as well—nothing. Now I was concerned. Luckily, I had my own key and let myself in. The dog settled itself comfortably on the doormat, patiently awaiting its next walk. I called out for Mum several times.

Maybe she had gone out, but it was unusual for her not to have drawn the curtains. I dragged myself up the stairs to her bedroom. The door was ajar. I knocked gently in case she was having a nap.

"Mum?"

No answer, and not even the sound of deep breathing. I pushed the door open slowly. The scene that met my eyes took time to register with my brain. Everything had slowed down. I heard the letter-box rattle, letters falling on the mat, and the dog barking, all from a long way away.

My mother was lying on the bed in a dark lake of deep red. Her entrails trailed over the bedside, and the contents of her throat were clearly visible where it had been hacked to pieces. A large knife was protruding from her chest. I stood staring at the knife and remembered it was the carving knife with its yellowed ivory handle. I wanted to be back in bed, fast asleep, deep in my hangover. Vomit rose in my throat. For some reason, I turned away from my mother so she should not see me being sick.

I trembled as I got out my mobile and phoned the police.

The next few days were a living nightmare. The police took me to the station to make a statement, and I told them all that had happened since I'd woken up. But the detective inspector seemed more interested in what I had been doing the night before. I told him as best as I could remember, although, after the second bottle of wine, things had become hazy. I did manage to remember that I had collapsed fully dressed on the bed at the end of the evening. The inspector nodded.

"Must have been a bit of a strain looking after her all those years."

'No, she was my mum. After Dad died, she went to pieces a bit, but I never minded a bit looking after her. In fact, over the last year, she's been great. I mean, she was getting really better."

"Bit of strain on the ol' marriage, though, wasn't it? Going to see mum every day. Leaving your wife to do all the work."

I protested that, of course it wasn't. That wasn't the way our marriage worked. We were perfectly happy. But the inspector and the accompanying sergeant were already rising from their seats.

The sergeant read me my rights, and there and then, I was charged with murder. Arriving at the trial was hell: people battering the police van where I was held hand-cuffed to a plastic seat and then the verbal abuse as I was led into court with a blanket over my head.

The trial didn't last long. My fingerprints were all over the knife even though my lawyer had pointed out in my defense that I did the carving when we had our Sunday roast at my mum's. But my jacket was the clincher. The stain I had mistaken for wine was my mother's dried blood, and hairs that had been viciously ripped from her head were found in the pocket. It tied in with my wife's statement. She maintained we had argued and she had slept in the spare room and had heard me go out in the early hours and then return a while later. There were traces of blood in the bathroom where I must have washed myself. Even I began to believe I might have done the awful thing in some kind of alcoholic stupor.

I was given life (15 years with parole). I won't go into the details of the abuse I suffered over the years I spent in prison and the constant threat that I was going to be "done in properly" or my constant thoughts of suicide, which I never carried through because I knew deep down it would be seen as an admission of guilt.

Time passed, and there came a day when I was free. The prison officer disdainfully handed me the few belongings I had left. In fact, they were the only things I had left. Sheila, to universal approval, had divorced me and married Keith. Everything I had owned they now possessed. Evidently, all my money and assets belonged to the business company that Sheila and Keith had set up together.

I wondered which one of them had done the actual murder or if they had done it together. It didn't really matter; I had resigned myself long ago in prison that I would never be able to prove my innocence.

The prison officer handed me the last item on the list, my bracelet, which I noticed was face side up again.

"You can keep that," I said.

"Sorry, sir" - he managed somehow to make the word *sir* sound like a swear word - "but you have to take everything that you came in with."

I left the prison. I knew where I would head first. The charity shop was still there, and the same old man, who didn't seem to have aged a jot, was behind the counter.

I handed him the bracelet.

"I'd like to donate this, please."

"That's very kind of you, sir."

I left the shop as I watched him carefully put a price ticket on it and place it under the glass counter. I watched outside for a few moments and then, to my astonishment and horror, saw Sheila and Keith approaching the shop. I turned up my collar and bowed my head, but they obviously didn't recognize me. I looked like a tramp, which, in effect, I was. So I looked through the window as they browsed around the shop. Then I saw Sheila grab Keith's arm and point excitedly to something in the glass counter. I watched as the old man took out my old bracelet with the token still attached and handed it to them. They bought it immediately, and I caught an expression of ecstasy as she placed it around Keith's wrist. I started to shuffle away before they exited the shop, but I took just one last look.

The old man was staring straight at me with his penetrating, cat-like green eyes. I couldn't say for sure if there was a slight smile on his lips, but I did notice something I had overlooked before. He had quite distinct Chinese features.

WHITE RABBIT

The trip had gone bad. It had never happened to him before, but he had heard about such things from others. He wanted to get out of the discotheque as fast as possible, even if it meant leaving with the woman dressed in red on his arm. He would probably have to go to bed with her, but it was preferable to the nightmare version of reality he was experiencing. He knew he shouldn't have scored those tabs. He should have stuck with the old California Sunshines or, even better, his personal favorites: Pyramids. He had always had great trips on Pyramids.

FLASHBACK: "*No*," Mickey said. "*These are better. The real deal. White Rabbits, direct from Amsterdam. Blow your fuckin' mind. Just got them in, and they're going fast.*"

He should have been suspicious when he had found out that Mickey had nothing else, but Mickey was usually safe. It was his own fault, he decided. He should never have dropped two. He had never taken two tabs before. But they had looked so small and harmless. His first trip had only been half a Pyramid, and it had been the best.

He had lost track of time when he'd dropped the first one. That was the worst of it. He had lost track of time and could not get it back. Got to get back on track...track...track...The thought echoed around his mind until it disappeared like the sound of a clunking stone dropped down a well. He tried to pull it back, but it had gone.

He remembered he had taken the first one back at his bedsit, and then suspecting he'd been ripped off, as nothing seemed to be happening, he had dropped a second. He had kept on looking at his digital watch, trying to work out the time between the first and second tabs. The dial had made no sense to him. Neither had the numbers, which seemed to be running backwards. Had he set the watch that way? He couldn't remember then, and he couldn't remember now, and he knew he really should—it was something important. He knew the countdown was one of the features of the watch, but now he could not remember what it was set for, or even how you set it.

The useless tabs had started giving him a headache. The four walls of his tiny bedsit, instead of providing their usual comforting solidity, seemed to be closing in on him. The smallness of the place was oppressing him, making him feel claustrophobic. It was as if he had suddenly got too large for the place.

What the hell had Mickey sold him? he remembered thinking at the time. He'd decided he needed some fresh air. He usually preferred to stay at home when he was tripping, watching the box and listening to some sounds, but then, on an impulse, he'd decided to go to the discotheque. It had seemed important at the time. He had hoped the strobes and the cacophony of music and special effects would set him off on a trip, if it really was acid, that is, and then he could return home and do his usual stuff.

The discotheque was called *Flamingos*, and the outside was painted a luminescent shade of pink. He had gone there a few times pissed-up. It was the first time on a trip, or *possible* trip.

Something was wrong. He sensed it before he saw it. Not only had the place been repainted an even stronger shade of pink but the sign had been changed to *Flamingos 2000*.

The bouncer had taken his fiver and nodded him through wordlessly. The place had seemed a lot busier and manic than usual - the bar was four or five deep - and he had skipped getting a drink and mingled with the writhing crowd on the thick glass dance floor.

The floor was made up of hundreds of lit squares that constantly changed in color and intensity. It mesmerized him. He stared down at his feet, which seemed to be embedded in the light, and as he moved them in time to the pulsing beat of the music, it seemed as if they controlled the changes in the rhythm. It was at that moment he had realized he was tripping, and he was coming up really quickly—faster than he could control. He had felt like laughing when the whole meaning of his wristwatch running backwards and the change in the sign had become clear: it was, of course, the millennium! The whole point of scoring the acid had been to celebrate the New Year in the warmth and security of his little bedsit with a nice trip. And then it all went bad...

FLASHBACK - He reluctantly drew his eyes away from the mesmerizing floor and saw that all the people around him were dancing in perfect synchronicity with him, the lights, and the music, but they had become translucent, clockwork robots with grinning grey skulls. They were staring at him. They had recognized he was different! The grinning skulls turned in unison to examine him. Then the bubbles started to fall on him. He had forgotten about the bubble machine. He stared at one

coming down from the ceiling. It was huge and seemed to take forever before it landed somewhere out of sight. The robot people were on to him! They had sent the bubble, just like the huge bubble that appeared in *The Prisoner* TV series whenever Number Six tried to escape from the Village. He had no doubt that the bubble would wrap itself around him until it engulfed him completely. He would be entrapped.

He had to get off the dance floor. Escape. Get out of the place. A part of his brain kept reminding him that he was having a bad trip and he should not bring attention to himself. The thought awakened his usually insipid paranoia.

Every time he tried to get off the dance floor, his feet became leaden, but he found if he concentrated hard enough on the fact that he was tripping, the whole place would flashback to some sort of normality for a moment. It was whilst in one of those grabbed moments of reality that he realized how strongly he wanted, and needed, a drink. A double whisky might take the edge of the bad acid.

As he thought of bad acid, a message came over the Tannoy system. He recognized it from his live *Woodstock* album—the disc jockey was warning everybody about some bad acid that was being circulated. He was using the exact words that had been used at *Woodstock*.

Was the disc jockey also in on it? That message couldn't be right, he told himself, and he forced himself to listen hard. He concentrated and heard the words properly; it was not a message about bad acid being circulated—it was the disc jockey reminding everyone that there were just two hours to go until midnight.

It seemed to take ages to reach the bar. He kept on looking at the numbers on his watch to check on how long he was taking to get there, but he could no longer remember if the numbers were running forwards or backwards. In fact, the watch made no sense at all. As soon as he had the thought that the numbers might be running backwards, the people around him also started moving backwards, as if on rewind. Was this his first or second visit to the bar? he asked himself.

FLASHBACK: A barmaid in a pink bunny girl outfit was playing with her little white tail, asking him what he wanted to drink. He heard a voice saying, "Double whisky, please," in a very loud drawl. The bunny girl reacted immediately and, in the blink of an eye, had set the drink before him and was handing him his change.

He swallowed some of the whisky. The taste was familiar. He decided it must be his second drink. He was pleased he was getting some sort of hold on his bearings. A voice disturbed this moment of serendipity.

The voice belonged to a young woman in a glaringly red dress—Alice.

FLASHBACK: "Thanks," she mouthed. Her teeth looked sharp, and she flicked her tongue in and out of her garish red hole of a mouth like snakes. The sound of her voice hit him some moments afterwards.

He found that he was withdrawing his hand from a glass he had just handed her. She fancied him, he remembered, and then he remembered they were waiting for a slow number to come on so they could rub themselves against each other. He was putting his mouth to her ear, and she was nodding and grinning. And then drawing his head to hers, she shouted in his ear. The breath from her mouth was so hot it burnt his cheek.

FLASHBACK: "You're off your head." Her words came warmly in his ear like trickling, hot honey. "Off off off off offffff head head head headdddddd."

Then the record that she had been waiting for came on. It was "Lady in Red," a record he profoundly hated. He remembered something. She had told him that it was her favorite, and she had requested it and, no doubt, dressed for it. They played a stupid game at her suggestion—guessing the color of each other's underwear. She went first. She was right, he said, although now he couldn't remember what color she had said his underwear was, although he would have agreed to any color. In fact, he wasn't sure he was wearing any. His turn. He was pretty sure he had told her that she was wearing red knickers to go with the red fishnet stockings, a complete tart's outfit. It was a no-brainer, really, as everything she was wearing was red—including the heart-shaped pendant around her neck. She had told him that that was for her to know and for him to find out.

FLASHBACK: Gross, scissor-like smile again, and a whiff of alcohol-laden breath. He caught the strong, salty-sea smell of her sweat as she moved. Somehow he knew that was how her cunt smelt.

That was why he had a throbbing down below. He couldn't tell if he was big down there or small. He daren't look. At least things were beginning to make sense, he reassured himself again. Perspective was forming.

FLASHBACK: She was in his arms, dancing.

Was he rewinding or fast-forwarding? They stumbled around, clinging to each other, and grinding their hips together in slow motion to the music. She was thrusting so hard against him he could feel her pelvic bone.

FLASHBACK: The robots were back. They were both now part of a huge, erotic, robot waltz.

She pulled away briefly. She was looking down at his trousers. He followed her gaze to the bulge there. "I know," she was saying, clicking her teeth, which were getting sharper by the minute. "Don't worry, I'll take care of that later." She patted it with her robot hand, and then ground her hips against him again. A sensation of flooding warmth filled his testicles. He wasn't sure, but out of the corner of his eye, he was sure that her features had grown considerably older. She was dribbling from her ancient cracked lips and toothless gums. She leant forward, and much to his horror, she breathed on him. Aimless laughter cackled through the air from her wrinkled throat.

She was laughing, and she put her enormous ear to his mouth. "You've given me a hard on." It was his voice, but the words were coming from her ears as he drew his lips towards them.

"I asked for this," she said, pulling him to the dance floor.

FLASHBACK: "I love this record." Her words hummed in his ear. "Let's dance."

Once again, he was going backwards in time. She drew back. Her skull grinned at him. The empty eye sockets were regarding him even though there were no eyes. Then he spotted them. They were hanging on her cheeks, connected by wires. She sucked them back into their sockets with a slurp. He could now see all her veins throbbing throughout her translucent, robot body as it pumped blood to all its parts. The clockwork wheels were turning in her head, spewing out thoughts. He could see the thoughts running through her brain on ticker tape. The instructions on the tape were too small for him to read. He watched in silent horror as his name, Al, was fed through the clockwork mechanism of her brain. He tried to scream, but he had a sinking feeling that only his jaw had dropped. He was gaping and gulping like a landed fish.

FLASHBACK: Time switched. Time stopped running backwards, and they were back in what he now considered must be the present.

They were both drinking, anonymous amongst the heaving crowd. She slyly stroked the throbbing down below, making it more urgent. More information came to him. More perspective. He calmed down. Some sort of reality was returning—no more robots. He ordered cocktails at her suggestion, two Long Island ice teas.

They were all set to celebrate the millennium, and then they were going to go back to her place, where she was going to *take care* of his throbbing. For a moment, he felt like smiling, but it must have been a grin. He had no control over his features. She was giving him a strange look. Was his face stuck? It felt like it. Had a spring broken in his clock head?

FLASHBACK: "Out of your head," she mouthed at him. "Off off off off offfffff head head head headddddd." The words cascaded around him, falling in no particular order like a flipped deck of cards.

Now they were crunched up together on a velvet-covered sofa, sipping the cocktails through straws. They were sharing a joint with an old man who had an enormously long neck.

FLASHBACK: The old man's face was gradually melting like a Salvador Dali clock. It melted across the table and onto the floor.

The countdown started. He knew what she expected of him. He obediently obliged. He didn't want to stand out. The robots must not notice him. They huddled together and started kissing.

FLASHBACK: Her tongue was a slimy eel, desperately trying to slide down his throat towards his testicles.

People were cheering. They were oblivious to the noise as they explored each other's mouths, sending coded sexual messages with their tongues. They released each other and, by mutual agreement, got ready to leave. His hard-on insisted on it. His penis pushed urgently against his trousers, demanding the release of a pent-up flood.

She guided him through the heaving crowd which was threatening to become robotic again. Her hand was sweaty and urgent. He let her pull him, secretly pleased by her debauched, open desire to get him in her bed and between her legs.

They were at her place in no time. They moved at twice the speed of normal, slow-motion people, strobing along the pavement, hardly seeming to touch it. The large, studio-type room she had led him into was dim, and he could barely make out the objects. One piece of furniture was prominent— the bed. There were piles of unwashed garments strewn over it, and across the floor. He knew they are unwashed because the whole place stunk of them.

FLASHBACK: Female salty smells overlaid by a deep, deep musk. It was too strong. It made him want to gag.

He was used to bathing regularly and always changing into freshly laundered cloth, a task he accomplished himself. The clean red dress was a dirty lie. It was an exception rather than the rule. Before he could change his mind about sleeping with her, or even beginning a retreat, they were toppling onto the bed. Their clothes were quickly discarded. They seemed to fly off by themselves. She lay back, waiting, expecting to be kissed. He obliged. Her snake-like tongue wound its way inside his mouth. It was everywhere, exploring every cavity. It was urgent. He fondled a breast and sucked one of her nipples, trying not to breathe through his nose. Every time he did, he smelled her stinking sweat. This foreplay was expected of him, he knew. All he wanted to do now was get the whole thing over with. She made gasping sounds to show her appreciation and offered up her other breast to him. The nipple hardened in his mouth as he sucked. He traced a line with his tongue down from her breasts and her stomach. She sighed, making more gasping noises, letting him know she knew where he was heading and that was what she wanted.

FLASHBACK: She placed both hands on his head, ever so slightly pushing, pushing it down towards the musk-scented wetness between her legs.

His mouth was there, where she wanted it to be. He managed to stifle his sense of smell. He knew what was expected of him, and his tongue obliged. She shifted her weight and opened her legs wider. He glanced up and saw that she was holding her feet, pushing up her buttocks. Her tongue was unconsciously lolling out of her mouth, her eyes tightly shut as she concentrated on whatever pleasure he was conjuring from that stinking, steaming, wet hole that lay between her legs. She writhed, and groaned, pushing her wetness into his face. She spasmed, as she reached orgasm after orgasm. The musky stench was now overpowering. It was much worse than the unwashed clothes.

FLASHBACK: A ridiculous line from Frank Zappa beamed into his head: "Don't you ever wash that thing?"

The Zappa music swam lazily around his mind, gently nudging thoughts to the surface. He shut down his sense of smell as much as he could, trying to concentrate on Zappa's music in his head and licking the ever-escaping mollusc with the tip of his tongue, gentle strokes whilst he settled himself. But she did not want gentle. She was writhing furiously now, hips gyrating and bucking violently. It was difficult to maintain a grip. He came up for air.

He rolled to his side and checked with his hand down below. He was hard. She pulled him up and onto her, all pretence of feministic gentleness gone. She grunted and moaned like an animal nursing an open wound.

FLASHBACK: He was like a sack of potatoes, which she dragged up and over her body, organizing him into the right position.

In her greed and excitement to have him inside her, she fumbled as she put it in, and he slid out. She moaned and helped him get back inside her again. She was so wet now that they really didn't need to use their hands. His penis was now an extension of himself—a rock-hard heat-seeking missile. She let out a satisfactory snort, and her hotness enveloped him. A dribble of saliva ran down her cheek from the corner of her mouth.

He could not understand how he was still erect. Her whole being nauseated and disgusted him. It was as though, by the consummation of the act, he was cleansing himself. He set to with renewed vigor. The end was in sight, and she urged him on to that small death—the disintegration of the self.

He would briefly melt into her. She would hold him until all his seed was spent. She would grab his buttocks tighter, their bodies making slapping and sucking noises.

She was bucking and thrusting against him, urging him on.

He was just glad to be away from the stench and able to breathe. He pushed hard and fast. He wanted to get this over with as quickly as possible. Zappa's discordant jazz notes urged him remorselessly onwards. He wondered if he would have an orgasm and what it would be like on acid. Would it make him better, stop the bad trip? It didn't seem like an orgasm was coming, but they were definitely building up to something. He was trying desperately to hold onto his place within her writhing body. It was difficult, and several times, it slipped out. Her hand was there, quick as a flash, to put it back in. God, he wanted this to end so much. It was expected of him now. He could sense that. Should he fake it? He had never faked an orgasm before. How did one go about it?

The more sensible part of his brain was telling him: *Of course not, stupid! She'll know you faked it.* He had to agree with his sensible self.

FLASHBACK: How to stop it, then? to come or not to come? that was the question. He could not stop stupid phrases forming in his mind.

The stupidity of his situation made him want to laugh, but he knew that would be rude. She would definitely take it the wrong way. He slowed down, and she did so in turn, probably mistakenly thinking he wanted to prolong the awful experience. She must have had her orgasm by now, or perhaps she had faked it? It wasn't fair. The smell of her sex assaulted him. It was coming from every pore of her being. The slower rhythm helped him to think. He avoided kissing her by breathing heavily into her ear. Something was starting to happen to him. He pulled her closer to him, and she complied willingly, hissing and sucking her teeth in expectation. His hand cupped her buttocks. She was definitely expecting him to finish and was making encouraging noises to urge him on. She swore in his ear and slapped his buttocks. She probably thought she was being sexy, though the fact that she was so crude in her expectations did make him want to finish. Something was definitely going to happen.

FLASHBACK: He felt himself getting bigger.

He was tangled up in a deckchair on the beach. The dawn was coming up over the sea. The lady in red was nowhere to be seen. How he had managed to get there, he did not know. Time had jumped again, and he didn't know if he was in the future or the past. He disentangled himself from the chair. He could still smell her on his fingers, so she was in the past, and he the present. The smell reminded him of her unwashed vagina. It was disgusting, and it made him want to throw up. He was tempted to wash in the sea, but the tide was out, and the rocks looked slippery. He would get home fast and give himself a good scrub in the little sink in his room. He felt an urgent need to get home now. Very urgent. He wanted to get there before the town started to wake up. He could hear it begin to stretch and yawn with car noises and shop deliveries starting. Luckily, his place was not far.

FLASHBACK - He turned up the collar on his jacket *so I felt like an actor, And I thought of Ma, and I wanted to get back there, your face, your race, the way that you talk, I kiss you, you're beautiful, I want you to walk, we've got five years, stuck on my eyes, five years, what a surprise, we've got five years, my brain hurts a lot.*

His brain hurt as well, now that he thought about it, because he could not stop David Bowie's "Five Years" playing in his head as he walked fast, his head down. He avoided the main roads, sticking to the side roads and some alleyway shortcuts he knew.

He was home. It felt so safe. All he wanted was to take his clothes off, wash, and get into bed.

He took off his button-down shirt and dark green vest. He noticed there was a large dark stain on the front of the vest. It felt sticky. He put it in the sink to soak. He watched as the sink filled with water and the water gradually became pinker as it stained the white porcelain red.

FLASHBACK: Crimson letters accumulated in the water until they formed legible words. He recognized a line from Macbeth. *No, this my hand will rather the multitudinous seas incarnadine, making the green one red.*

The missing parts in his recollection of the night's events fell into place, a cascade of flash-cards falling like red rain onto the green velvet of his memory.

THE WOMAN IN THE BURKA

She sat directly opposite from me while we were on the tube. Her eyes were downcast most of the time, but that was not surprising. Nobody makes eye contact on the underground. You read a book or the free Metro newspaper, listen to music on your telephone or iPod with your eyes closed, or gaze vaguely into the distance, like a really old person sitting in a deckchair and staring out to sea—anything to avoid eye contact. I'm sure it must be worse for women, with some men just making eye contact with their busts or legs. On top of that, she was wearing a full burka, so she was getting hostile stares from several of the passengers. Muslims were not exactly popular at that moment. Isis had just committed the worst terrorist attack in twenty-first century Europe's history in Paris, and the population of London was still in a state of shock and fear. Wearing a burka on the Victoria line in the middle of rush hour was probably not a wise fashion choice, even if it was your religion and you respected it.

My eyes were drawn to her as if the burka held a magnetic force all of its own. I knew I wasn't the only one. Other eyes in the carriage were upon her, shining like lasers, and some were notable for the open malice they contained. A skinhead with a swastika tattooed in the middle of his forehead, a la Charles Manson, was deliberately staring maliciously at her, obviously willing her to look back at him so he could intimidate her more. I, too, avoided the skinhead's eyes. I did not want to be a companion in his racist hatred (I disliked racism intensely; I had suffered enough of it myself, enough not to want to attract it), but I felt something—a stirring, a flicker of recognition: the capacity for violence propelled by paranoia.

In normal circumstances, I would have felt sorry for the woman. But these were not normal circumstances, and how could I even tell if it was a woman? The burka made the form underneath the clothing indistinguishable, and I could only just make out the eyes under the veil, which might be the only clue. They were brown, practically black, but they could have been a man's or a woman's. She, if it was a she, kept her head lowered most of the time, only raising it occasionally to glance at the passing stations. Where was she heading? My guess was the end of the line—Brixton, like me. I looked at the feet. They were small, but were they small enough to definitely be a woman's? I decided she had to be a woman. I had never heard of a jihadist (if, indeed, that was what he/she/it/ was) disguising himself as a woman. I realized suddenly I was making uncalled-for preconceptions. It was wrong, terribly wrong.

Why didn't she at least keep her head raised and just close her eyes? It wasn't as if you could see much of them under that veil. It was as if she were wearing sunglasses. Her arms were crossed, and her hands were folded flat under each other. Were they hiding something? On her lap was a large hand-bag. The bag would disguise any movement she made with her hands. Had she deliberately placed it in that position? I could swear that the bag was moving slightly, or was it her hands trembling beneath it? Could it really be a suicide bomber? Now I knew I was definitely starting to get paranoid.

But judging by the looks of my fellow passengers, I was not the only one.

The train stopped at Warren Street. As usual, not many people got on or off. I found myself willing her to get off, for the sake of my nerves, if nothing else. But she sat quite still, her head alternately staring straight ahead or bent as if in prayer. I started to think: which station would I choose if I were a suicide bomber on the Victoria line? I instinctively knew the answer: Victoria itself. It would cause the most carnage and chaos. I put the terrible thought out of my mind. Instead, I focused on the inner problem of my conscience.

Had I really suddenly become some sort of racist? I had always deplored such people. Just because a woman was wearing a burka, it did not mean she hated the West; it just meant she respected her religion. What was wrong with that? Except that religious ideology can be taken too far. And now, with the advent of the Islamic State, it had. Ordinary people were now frightened and suspicious of anything remotely Islamic.

A couple sitting near me were whispering in each other's ears, but not low enough that I could not make out the hushed words "Transport Police." We were nearing Victoria station. Now the stares were not just coming from our carriage. Word seemed to have spread. People were already getting up from their seats, and they were deliberately queuing at the far-end carriage doors, as far away from the suspicious woman as possible. There was even a crush forming. There were always a lot of commuters getting off at Victoria, and the middle double doors were usually favorite exit points, but they were near the woman in the burka. She was sitting on the seat right next to the middle exit door on the left of the carriage, the side the doors opened at Victoria.

She did not move from her seat. With a feeling of dread, I watched for any movement of her hands. People hurriedly got off, and other people hurriedly got on. The warning beeps sounded, and the doors closed on the freshly boarded passengers. The train moved off with a slight jerk. I now felt sure that she was going all the way to Brixton. I wondered about getting off at the next station Pimlico, or moving to another carriage. Would being in another carriage protect me from a bomb blast? Probably not, I concluded. We were near the front of the train. It would just mean I would be probably be burnt alive, die of smoke inhalation, or be crushed. None of them sounded particularly appetizing. I still remember the horror of King's Cross. You could smell the smoke for weeks afterwards. It lingered there no matter how much the place was ventilated. It was a macabre reminder of the horror that had taken place in that underground mass grave. Every passenger at that time moved faster through Kings Cross than any of the other stations. That dreaded smell always seemed to cling to ones clothes for hours afterwards. Why was I thinking all these macabre things? I tried to make my mind blank and concentrate on my breathing. That was supposed to calm you.

The new passengers who had got on at Victoria had not had the time to take in the scenario, and the empty seats by the side of the woman in the burka were soon occupied. It was not for long, though. People discreetly moved seats or got up to stand by the exit doors. The woman in the burka seemed not to notice. She kept her eyes pointed rigidly ahead. I could imagine her jaw set just as firmly underneath the veil. She must have felt the animosity surrounding her like a physical presence, pressing in on her from all sides as if a vice of pure hatred was trying to squeeze the life out of her and her religion.

I closed my eyes. I could not bear to watch anymore. At every stop, my heart thundered in my chest. Then, eventually, after the few stops in between the end of the line, we neared Brixton. There was the inevitable stop in the darkness of the tunnel before reaching the station proper. I had made the journey so many times that the small delay was practically a ritual part of any Brixton trip. It always seemed fairly innocuous. I usually used the small space of time to see if I had left anything and to collect my thoughts. But today the short wait seemed interminable. Even the driver's reassuring voice that we would be on the move again shortly seemed full of doom. The woman was starting to fidget now and seemed to grab the bag more firmly. And I was becoming more and more unsettled.

It was just as we had pulled into Brixton that it happened. Three men suddenly launched themselves into the carriage. All three were dressed in dark track-suits.

One of them yelled in the loudest voice I had ever heard, "SAS! Everyone on the floor."

Another of the men put a large gun against the woman's head.

"Not you! You don't move a finger!" he shouted in her ear.

As I threw myself to the floor, I caught a glimpse of her trembling uncontrollably. She wasn't the only one. Everyone in the carriage was shaking with fear. I think everyone thought they were going to die.

The SAS man shouted at the woman in the burka to raise her hands very slowly and place them behind her head. His voice seemed to fill the carriage. She did as she was told. I felt like shutting my eyes but found I couldn't. It was as if I were hypnotized; I just couldn't tear my eyes away from the scene that was unfolding before my eyes. Any second, I expected to see the woman's brains splattered against the carriage's window. Another of the men tentatively put the barrel of his pistol against the bag and lifted the flap. Then the most incongruous sight in the world met my eyes. I think it was probably the same for the SAS men, hardened as they were. The tiny head of a kitten poked its way out. It gave out a pathetic little squeak.

I suppose in any other situation, say, if I were watching a movie, it would have been extremely funny. But this was real life, and I was close to shitting myself.

The SAS man stared at the kitten in disbelief. "What the fuck is this? Some kind of sick joke?"

Finally, in the ominous silence, the woman in the burka said, "It's cat. I take for injections. Did not know if they allow on underground."

"What else is in the bag?" the SAS man demanded.

"Blanket for cat and purse." She moved one of her arms as if she were going to show him.

"Don't move a muscle, or I'll blow your fucking brains out!" The SAS man shouted at her.

One of the other SAS men ordered us out of the carriage. We didn't need to be asked twice. Brixton station was full of transport police and men in what looked like bloated khaki spacesuits. I guessed they were the bomb squad. Perhaps they were going to defuse the kitten. The ridiculous thought, mixed with relief, made me giggle out loud. One of the policemen gave me an odd look.

"You're in shock, mate," he said, taking me by the arm and escorting me up the escalator into a waiting ambulance.